But We Are Exiles

Laurentian Library 45

But We Are Exiles

A NOVEL BY

Robert Kroetsch

MACMILLAN OF CANADA TORONTO

First published in 1965
First Laurentian Library edition 1977

ISBN 0-7705-1508-8

Printed in Canada for
The Macmillan Company of Canada Limited
70 Bond Street, Toronto M5B 1X3

To Mary Jane

But We Are Exiles

The line in Peter's hands came taut just then; a chill shuddered up into his arms and aching neck. He heard himself yell and the skipper stopped pointing a finger into his own throat as if to make himself throw up and instead cut off the outboard motor with a turn of a thick wrist; the canoe began to swing downstream, bow first, anchored by the quarter-inch line in Peter's hands: 'Pull him in!' the skipper shouted in the sudden silence, the motor popping and then dead.

Peter gave a jerk, another, to set the hooks, his stomach going queasy, and now the grappling-hooks and line and whatever it was they had snagged began to come up, heavy, still too far down to be seen in the sun-filtering green and then dark of the water; the line curled dripping around his high-topped boots as if to entangle him; the wet, cold line stiffened his fingers.

And bent over he could feel the stillness strike the back of his bare head, half knocking life into him, half knocking it out. His breath came in lumps. He glanced up at the breath-tripping hush; at the broad river, mirror-smooth in the afternoon sun; at the old riverboat where she lay tied up beside her two black steel barges. No one had seen the canoe stop. The lifting bow bobbed gently. He looked down again at the water and this time saw his own face watching him; the prematurely balding blond head, the full lips and squinting deep-set eyes suggesting a moodiness that didn't belong with his tall and hard body. He studied the reflection as if not sure whom he might see.

The image mimicked his hesitation, mocked his doubt by repeating it. The deep-set eyes worried against the slant of light. The mouth, pursed and offering a kiss, in its subtle retreat, threatened now to open and drown. Peter shook his head to be sure it was himself he saw. A drop of water from the rising line scarred the face, exploded its frail composure.

The grappling-hooks swam into view. They did not bring up from the darkness Michael Hornyak, burned and dead and already a little soggy — 'Goddamnit,' the skipper said — but a water-logged stump; a deadhead that had drifted a thousand, fifteen hundred miles perhaps, water-carried from the edge of civilization, scoured and battered and soaked until it had sunk here in the Mackenzie River below a pier in a stretch of slack water off Norman Wells.

'Get that thing off your hooks and let's go for some coffee.' The skipper, slouched and baggy-eyed, gestured toward the M.V. *Nahanni Jane* where she lay tied up outside her barges at the end of the rock-fill pier. 'My skull's going to bust wide open from the goddamned fumes from this goddamned kicker.' He pulled the motor alive with one try.

'Wait!' Peter yelled.

There was something — an electric light socket and tin

2

shade, like the head of an oversize reading-lamp — caught in the roots of the deadhead.

'To hell with it,' the skipper shouted over the frantic whine of the kicker.

'Hold on!' Peter twisted the lamp free; he dropped it into the bottom of the canoe. The bulb had been broken out of the socket; the cord was gone. He jerked again and for a moment the naked three-pronged grappling-hooks glinted clean in the afternoon sun. He watched as the deadhead vanished; the upside-down sky undulated and then shattered away from the lifting and swinging bow.

The riverboat had lain tied up in Norman Wells for nearly four days with most of the crew loafing, then drunk, while the short, precious autumn turned to winter. The *Nahanni Jane* had one more downriver trip to complete; five hundred miles to run to the Arctic coast; eleven hundred miles to crawl back, bucking the Mackenzie's freezing current, then crossing Great Slave Lake before the half-breed crew members could scatter along the river and the whites could board a plane for the flight south to the stuccoed and mortgaged bungalows and the rented back-rooms and beer-parlours they called home. The boat was to be delivered to Yellowknife, where Michael Hornyak's new fishing company was to take over and turn her into a fish-packer. She was too old and too small to compete with the riverboats that Northern Transportation and Yellowknife Transportation were building. But the crew had a pride that scorned the fish-packers with their stink of whitefish and lake-trout entrails, their glitter of fish-scales, and their swarms of fat flies and fat Japanese and Indian women wielding quick bright knives while the boat went nowhere.

The great Hornyak himself, young baron of the trade that supplied frozen fish to Chicago and New York, had come flying in to Norman Wells yesterday to keep the *Nahanni Jane* moving. Only now the search for his body might tie her up for additional days. And even while the crew searched they were pleased as well as horrified, as if assured that a strange justice of some sort still prevailed.

' . . . so you see' — the chief engineer pointed brusquely at the man-hole over the compartment in which the explosion had occurred — 'the broken glass is right down there at the foot of the ladder.' Bill Arnafson was a short, stocky, middle-aged man with pale reddish skin and the bent beak of his cap pulled low over his red eyes as if he had been in engine-rooms so long that daylight blinded him. 'Somehow he smashed the light-bulb while he was coming through the man-hole; he got caught in the burst of flame like he was in a blow-torch.'

'Where did he get a lamp to begin with?'

Arnafson agreed defensively with the skipper: 'I should have had the damned thing locked up. I realize that.'

An oil-worker spoke in the group of men surrounding the man-hole: 'We could all get killed. The man who gave it to him ought to be hanged.'

The muscles of Captain McAlpine's square jaw began again their little dance of distress, the pot-belly he had developed through the summer sagging forward and down as he forgot for the moment to hold it sucked in. 'And he will be hanged, by God, if he was one of my crew.' He looked around the circle of men; but everyone was looking at the lamp held at arm's length by the chief.

'This thing is a false lead,' the chief said. 'I mean — this lamp could be off any one of a dozen boats or barges. It wouldn't rust in that cold water — '

'It could have been there all summer.' The skipper, with a grunt of relief, snatched the lamp away from the chief and forced it back into Peter's hands. 'For a few summers even. I saw a truck that went through the ice, and four years later they fished it out and put in some gas and hooked on a battery and drove away. I just want the simple facts. The bare unvarnished facts to send to the head office. Hornyak was interfering in something that wasn't his business.'

'Even if he did buy the boat,' Peter said.

4

'Captain, she's in my cabin.' Angi Boyle, the boat's cook, noticed the lamp in Peter's hands. Peter saw her big, rough hands go up to her cheeks; he checked an impulse to heave the lamp over the bow of the barge.

'The hard facts,' McAlpine repeated.

'I saw him with my own two eyes,' the cook confessed, wincing; the flesh of her full breasts picked up the motion and made it a shudder. 'He had a light cord wrapped around him, with a lamp on the end of the cord, when he jumped into the river.'

'Then there would have been a cord on the lamp.' The beak of Arnafson's cap nodded vigorously. 'Like I've been saying — that isn't my lamp — ours — at all. We can't start blaming ourselves, Skipper.'

'She's here,' the cook insisted, trying once more to get a hearing.

McAlpine ignored her, but now he noticed the Eskimo boy sitting on a bollard beside two empty oil-drums on which was set the air pump. The long rubber hose ran to a mask and the mask was a black blob of melted rubber. 'You were running the air-pump, Jimmie. What did you see?'

The oil-workers backed away, giving the boy room. They were a group of whites and half-breeds, dressed in yellow hard-hats, rubber boots for the mud, and muddy denim clothing. They waited. But Jimmie Kartuk shook his head. 'I wasn't running the pump. I was working on the reefer' — he pointed to the big, square, wooden refrigerator on the starboard side that made the barge list slightly — 'and the pilot was looking after the pump.'

'Jonas?'

Kartuk ignored the question. He'd signed on in Fort Simpson, to replace a missing deckhand, only because he'd missed his own boat and wanted a ride down to his home on the coast. And now he wanted only to be left alone. 'The cord of the lamp was wrapped around his middle. And the lamp was hooked on his shirt pocket.' He indicated the left pocket of his own blue denim shirt.

The cook nodded her agreement.

'So he could keep both hands free.' Arnafson tipped up the beak of his cap and blinked his red eyes. He was sweating around his mouth. 'There. The lamp could have easily bumped the ladder.'

'But the air-pump, goddamnit.'

Kartuk pointed apologetically. 'Mr. Guy.'

The skipper indicated Peter with an upward thrust of his jaw that erased his extra chin. He stood with his fists on his hips and remembered now to suck in his belly. 'What the hell were you doing for entertainment all this time?'

Peter tucked the lamp under an arm. 'There were five more compartments full of alkylate fumes. I jumped ashore. I didn't see anything but the splash when he went off the bow. And the current took him under the barge before he could come up once. I ran for a canoe.'

'We heard it five miles away,' an oil-worker volunteered.

'We heard him,' Angi said. 'Me and Jimmie. We could hear him bumping along the bottom of the barge. After he jumped everything was dead quiet and we could hear him. Couldn't we, Jimmie?'

'I've had nightmares about those six compartments,' the mate said. 'They're some terrible treacherous, Skipper.'

'He didn't drop the lamp?' McAlpine turned again to the deckhand, not a little proud of the integrity and persistence of his inquest.

'The cord was wrapped around him so he couldn't,' the Eskimo boy explained. 'All I saw was his arm.' He made a slight gesture of futility. 'He had that tattoo on his left arm. Of a ship with lots of sails.' Someone in the crowd laughed. 'His clothes were just ashes. Still burning a little. When he tried to brush the burnt clothes off his arm all the skin came off too, like a sleeve, and there was that tattoo under the skin, on the whiteness, like.'

An inboard motor coughed into life and gargled out of sight behind the stern of the barge, then a Peterborough boat drift-

6

ed into view with three R.C.A.F. men aboard, manning dragging-hooks and pike-poles.

'She's here,' the cook repeated, her arms crossed now beneath her handsome big breasts.

'Who's *here*?' the skipper finally wanted to know.

'Mr. Hornyak's wife. She got in while you were out dragging. She's in my cabin now, and she won't let me in to see her and she won't eat.'

'Leave her be then.'

'But she arrived all alone. And so young-looking. *Somebody* ought to do something.'

'You're getting paid.'

'She won't let me into the cabin. I tried to tell her – '

'What did you tell her?'

'Tell her indeed. What did I tell her!'

The skipper with a quick gesture cracked two knuckles of his left hand. 'What the hell did you tell her, Angi?'

'Try and find out something on this boat. Just try. In three hours I haven't found out a thing that makes sense. And you haven't even radioed – '

'I'll radio when it's time.' The skipper started toward the cook as if to knock her down. 'I'm not going to lose my ticket because some damned fool came snooping around here and blew himself up. I can't stand guard over this damned boat like it's a prison or some damned thing. I've got a right to go ashore and have a drink, just like anybody else.'

'You can do what you please, Captain. I didn't – '

'I'll send out a message when we've got the body. When we can explain what happened. You just tend to your goddamned galley . . . ''

Peter, listening, even before he spoke knew he shouldn't have opened his mouth. Staying out of trouble had become his specialty in the past six years. He hadn't killed Hornyak, even if he hadn't explained about the lamp. Nobody wanted to admit any responsibility; the skipper nor the chief nor anyone else; nobody had to. 'I knew Hornyak.'

7

'You knew — ' The skipper and the chief spoke at the same time.

'Sort of. A few years ago.'

'And you knew his wife?'

'He wasn't married then.'

'Go talk to her anyhow. And take that lamp to hell out of here.'

'Maybe not me, Skipper — ' The knock of panic hammered through Peter's chest. 'I'll go back searching.'

'Just talk to her. Keep her calm.' McAlpine turned to the men around him. 'Get the hell out on that water. I'm going on radio sked at eight.'

There was room now for Peter to move. He nodded hastily to the cook and turned and, following, half pushed her across the barge, past the big reefer. The silence behind him made him look back; the men didn't meet his glance but looked away as if somone had called to them from land.

Norman Wells, on the east shore, was a row of silver oil-tanks and white barracks and old warehouses set against the low Franklin Mountains. Turning again, Peter caught a glimpse westward over the stern of the riverboat; Bear Island was a splash of yellow afloat on the darkening water. Four and a half miles away, across the Mackenzie, old Camp Canol was a deserted and rotting army camp, half disguised again in green and yellow forest, spilling a row of rotting wooden barges down to the sandy shore.

He and the cook stepped down onto the lower second barge and walked across the deck through a tangle of lines and four-inch hoses, past heaps of tarpaulined deck-freight; and then they walked down a short, steep, cleated ramp and onto the deck of the M. V. *Nahanni Jane*. The cook turned toward the stern and walked a few paces and stopped in front of the low door-way that led down three steps into the galley. She pointed briefly and without speaking up to the next deck and disap-peared, her hands vanishing with a flick from the horizontal bar above the steps. Her hands were rough from work, Peter noticed again. Yet she could be gentle with a man, in the middle of a lonely night. He kicked at the white paint flaking off a porthole that looked in on the engine-room.

He had quarrelled with Hornyak at the dinner table and after the quarrel he led Hornyak down there through the galley entrance, past the two old Vivians and the cranky generators and the mess that resulted when Arnafson went on one of the drunks that only ended when he got the DT's and began to scream about his wife. Peter took Hornyak down into the engine-room from the galley *and Hornyak bent over a bin of tangled extension cords and loose bulbs and rolls of tape and pulled out a lamp that had no wire mask protecting the bulb.*

Peter hesitated, then said nothing.

'Your old buddy', Hornyak said, 'needs some light, Guy. What do you say?'

Peter said nothing.

'Guy, you don't know your own mind.' Hornyak straightened his tie with a gesture that was partially a twitch. He then tucked the tie into his shirt before he laughed, as if he dared it to try and choke him. 'Sometimes I envy you. My trouble is I know my own mind. And that's a terrible thing.' He waved the lamp around at the shadowed silence of the engine-room. 'I know what I want. You see that, Guy? I know till I ache from my balls to breakfast. I know till I want to wring one shout from that jesusly silent throat of yours.'

And Peter turned now and with that same lamp under his arm started up the ladder and onto the next deck.

Hesitantly.

For on an afternoon like this — only it was a spring afternoon, and hot, and six years ago now — he first heard that other name. He was hitch-hiking west to work in one of the railway hotels in the Rockies. To be near Kettle Fraser, who had gone out by plane. And to make what he thought of as big money so he could go back to Ontario in the fall and finish his degree, for he was in a university more suited to his mother's maiden name than to his father's income — and as he stood drowsing in that hot spring sunshine six years ago a car, coming from the wrong direction, careered off the road in front of him and slammed to a halt a foot from where he landed when he jumped into the ditch. 'Where're you headed?' the driver grinned through the open window. An unshaven, dark-haired young man Peter's own age, one eye black and blue. 'West.' 'Jump in.' 'You're headed east.' 'Christ, Hornyak can turn this jalopy around.'

And for the next nine days Peter Guy was first scared and concerned and reluctantly drunk, and then fascinated, not only by Michael Hornyak but by himself, and then carefree and drunk with abandon, and after a while no longer some of the other things he had been, not a twenty-year-old virgin, for one evening they picked up a girl in Regina and took turns driving until they set her down in front of the bus depot in Medicine Hat, and no longer a stranger to the police, for they backed into a parked car in front of a diner and a policeman who was having a cup of coffee almost sobered them up in a jail near Calgary, except that the jailer sold Mike a twenty-six of cheap rye for thirty bucks, and for a while no longer penniless, for Mike had only to write a cheque and say, 'Hornyak would like some cash.'

And then one evening Peter Guy sobered up and found himself hitch-hiking again, leaving behind him Michael Hornyak, the girl he wanted to marry, the mountains, a room in a big hotel.

But he didn't go east again. He went into the north. He might have gone east to his sister's graduation from university, if he hadn't got so drunk in Fort Smith that the stewardess wouldn't let him board the plane. He might have gone home to his mother's funeral, but word got to him in Yellowknife three weeks after the burial. A month later in the mail he received a shoe-box full of old family photographs and one hundred shares in a railway that had gone bankrupt. He tried

10

three times to write his father an explanation; then he threw his legacy into the river.

'Come in,' he heard a voice say, jarring him back to the boat.

And it was the voice he had promised himself it would not be. For a moment it was not six years ago but yesterday, last night, and he braced himself not to open but to slam the door, lest Hornyak should be there too.

She did not turn around; she sat still on the pink wire chair beside the unmade bunk and its rumpled brown woollen blankets, her back to the door, the insides of her bare arms just visible and lightly tanned, her shoulders bare in the pale blue, sleeveless, and neatly ironed dress and well tanned and freckled slightly from a distant but warm September sun, her black hair neatly coiled as if she had never been to bed, her neck slender and bowed; and he remembered the holes in those beautiful ears, as if obedience to some pagan ritual had recommended the marring of their beauty and had succeeded only in making them more beautiful, even without the small pearl ear-rings she was wearing now; he remembered even after six years the way she had of letting one bare heel come out of a shoe when she was sitting still but nervous. And the heel was up now, the bright smooth skin of the arch familiar. Her right foot was hooked around a leg of the chair, like a little girl's, as if the bitch in the woman were momentarily asleep or invisible, though it meant her knees weren't quite together and it was nice to be sitting somewhere in a room where you could catch a glimpse of the soft white skin of the insides of her thighs, a glimpse of the darkness —

'Peter?' she said.

'I'm sorry.'

'Who killed him, finally?'

'Nobody.'

'But he led a charmed life. Sometimes I think — that was the one belief he had. That he was indestructible.'

'Nobody killed him.' Peter put a foot up onto the high sill,

11

the sill that was raised to keep out water in a storm. 'I was there.'

'But he's dead.'

'It was an accident. Honest to God.'

The Big Ben alarm-clock on the unpainted chest of drawers beside the foot the bunk ticked as if trying to speak. The white hands on the unglassed black face said it was four-thirty. He pulled the cabin door half shut behind him and stood on the raised sill with the back of his head hooked on the top of the door jamb, his hands in his pockets, the lamp under one arm, the palms of his hands beginning to sweat.

'Then you're his wife.'

'He didn't tell you?'

'I didn't suppose you two — '

'Widow,' she said. 'That Eskimo boy who met the plane wouldn't admit to speaking English so the cook woman had to tell me, and all I could think of was the word widow and how was I ever going to use it first, like when I was a girl and wanted to know what it felt like to say some bad word. And the cook kept waiting for me to cry or some damned thing.'

'She takes care of all of us.'

'She kept saying poor darling poor darling you mustn't cry and offering me coffee and blankets and pushing me into the cabin — and that poor darling business as if I somehow needed to be primed so I could play the role of the bereaved wife. And all I could think of was widow. Caroline Hornyak, widow. Kettle Fraser, aged twenty-six, childless, loverless, now husbandless. Nothing — '

She turned suddenly on the unlikely pink chair that had somehow got into the riverboat cabin and on which Peter himself and half the crew had sat down to pull off their boots before plopping stocking-footed and sometimes underweared onto the naked-from-the-belly-button down and not-a-little-hairy body of Angi Boyle, cook, well-meaning woman who might and who might not remember to collect a slight fee for services rendered, and whose greatest and inevitable compliment was well done, laddio, as if fornication itself was simply the doing to a turn of one more ham roast, one more turkey.

'My God, you're big,' she said.

He stepped off the raised door-sill and into the cabin and let the door swing shut. Anger swelled into his voice along with the faint resonance of desire. 'A growing boy, Mrs. Hornyak.'

'He didn't tell you he married me?' She was holding on her lap a large brown purse of alligator that seemed to weigh heavy on her thighs. Her hips in the tight blue skirt were fuller than he remembered. 'You did see him?'

'We spoke once, and our conversation was to the effect that I'm a river bum.'

'I'm so pleased he ended not liking you.'

'Did he like anything but Mike?'

'There were times when he liked me.'

Deliberately: 'He liked what you've got between your legs.'

Her wide dark eyes continued to study him. 'Pete, he's dead.'

'You aren't the only person who isn't crying. There's been a mutiny here since we learned he bought the boat, only he didn't live to find out.'

'And if he had the mutiny would have been over.'

'Except that he blew himself to hell.'

'Shut up, Pete.'

'His wife was coming in on the semi-weekly flight so he chose that time to crawl down into a barge and clean out the stink of alkylate.'

She glanced at the purse on her lap. 'It was an accident,' she said.

And then Peter noticed the knuckles of her hands, white, her hands gripping the clasp of the purse. 'I was there,' he said. He shook his head. 'We started loading aviation gasoline for Tuktuk — and it didn't pass the gum test.'

'But it was an accident,' she said.

'We had just pumped off. A couple days before. The barge

was contaminated and had to be cleaned. Only the crew was all drunk by that time – '

'He wanted a son.' Kettle started to gesture, then dropped her hands again to her purse. She caught the toe of a shoe around a leg of the chair. 'He wanted a son, Pete.' And Peter watched the soft flush rise in her cheeks, rise beneath the honey glow of her tan. He might have touched her; but she went on speaking: 'I went to three doctors.' She saw his impulse and said, 'They all said I seemed to be fine.'

'And what did they say about Mike?'

'He wouldn't go to doctors.'

'He had that fine way of believing that even he could only make tentative suggestions to Michael Hornyak, and with little hope of getting the desired response.'

'Peter, you're making speeches. You come in here with that old knot in your throat. Stop pretending it's Mike. You never blamed Mike. You didn't blame Mike then. I'm sure of that. You don't blame him now.'

'I don't understand why somebody didn't long ago kill – '

He would not answer when the knock came. Kettle raised both hands to her ear-rings and said a hello that was a question. A question and a request that whoever was knocking give her time to look respectable. The tone and the gesture made Peter push open the door.

'Here we go now.' Angi Boyle handed in a pot of tea and two mugs. Peter put down the lamp on the floor beside a small suitcase and took the pot and the two empty mugs. Angi was gone after she had a good look around at the cabin and at Kettle's face, but before Peter could say thank you.

'Thank you,' he said to nobody. And then: 'We've been drinking tea by the barrelful on this bloody boat ever since the skipper hired himself a female cook who had the perspicacity to go to bed with him one night in Yellowknife.' He pushed some jars and tubes of cosmetics onto a pile with his forearm and set down the pot and the two mugs on the chest of drawers. 'Thirsty?'

'Let me.' Kettle stood up and put her purse on the bare mattress on the top bunk. She lifted the lid of the brown porcelain pot and peeked. 'Give it a second.'

Peter stood awkwardly beside her. For a moment neither had anything to say or do. The floor was so small they were forced against each other. A small square window in the rear wall looked out over a tarpaulined lifeboat and a ventilator from the engine-room. The cabin was hardly longer than the bunk, and the cook's clothes were hung on nails beside the window in the narrow space between the foot of the bunk and the wall. The handles of suitcases stuck out from under the lower bunk. Three pairs of shoes, the pink chair, and the chest of drawers took up most of the floor. Peter tried to step backwards and kicked Kettle's small suitcase. 'How did you know it was me – at the door when I knocked?'

She poured tea into both mugs. 'I remembered the way you walk. The sound.'

'The hell you did.'

She caught a laugh in her throat. Her elbow brushed his bare arm as she turned to give him a mug. She offered him the mug handle first, her beautiful large hands cupping the mug's chipped bottom.

Awkwardly he accepted, her fingers touching his. They were both silent; then into the quiet of the cabin crashed the high-pitched whine of the motorboats that were dragging the river. Peter bent to glance out the back window.

Kettle picked up her mug. 'I went to your room up there that night in the mountains. But you were gone. You didn't leave any word. You had left.'

The simple statement left him bowed at the window and not seeing.

Kettle took a sip of tea. 'The cook was telling me what happened and just by accident mentioned Guy – and I said not Peter Guy? And after that I couldn't let her into the cabin.' She pushed open the door as if to look out at the river and the boats and the distant shore and far beyond that the sharp

15

high Carcajou Range of the Mackenzie Mountains, glistening white in a new coat of snow. 'Go away, please, Peter,' she said. 'Now.'

And before he closed the door he knew she was crying.

Jeremiah Pottle, the red-headed Newfoundlander mate, offered to bet anyone ten dollars spot cash that the corpse would rise of its own accord after three days. Arnafson replied with a list of bodies that had disappeared into this river and never been found — a Slavey Indian trapper who turned over in a ratting canoe near Roche-qui-trempe-a-l'eau, a deckhand off the *Radium Jack* who went out looking for his gloves one night and never came back (though his new gloves were found next morning on a capstan), an American Negro soldier who slipped while unloading pipe for a pipeline that was built through a mountain wilderness and then promptly scrapped. The mate went on insisting, and at noon three days later a deckhand and a man from Imperial Oil and the chief each collected ten dollars, and after that the first pilot, Jonas Bird, predicted that in such cold water it would take six days more. Fermentation in the stomach, he explained in the soft voice of an old Indian who had spent his life on the Mackenzie, would be slow in such cold water. He gave as an example two brothers whose scow broke up in a storm on Mills Lake and who were both caught in a Redknife fish-net nine days later. But no bets were placed. After three busy days the crew had thoroughly cleaned *Barge 301;* they had pumped on 86,000 gallons of Aviation 115/145, which was too much for the water stage in late September, yet hardly enough to show the dead and missing Michael Hornyak that they were a damned fine bunch of men.

For he was there driving them, insidiously, though five boats and crews dragging for as long each day as the sun and the thickening smoke from a forest fire would permit could not find the body. And when Peter suggested they delay for another afternoon, even for another hour, the skipper didn't mention the smoke but only said they had a boat to deliver to Yellowknife before freeze-up. He was become a man of purpose; or a man of Hornyak's purpose. He told the crew to hoist the lifeboat and the skiff aboard, for those also had been put into the search, and the shore crew broke the loading-lines.

Peter spun the wheel hard to starboard and reached back to one of the two brass handles of the telegraph and rang the starboard engine from slow ahead to full astern.

An oil-worker lifted the headline off a post on the pier. The gangplank was about to splash into the river when Pottle swore, and two deckhands, the white and the Eskimo boy, dragged it onto the deck of *301*. Then Pottle, conspicuous with his unruly red hair, raised both arms over his head once more and dropped them with an outward swing.

All four deckhands gathered now on the port barge to take one last look at the pier and the men and buildings before the wilderness resumed. The shore quickly drifted away and began to be swallowed up in the dense smoke. For two days a forest fire burning unfought somewhere to the north-west had blanketed the river and camp in a smoke so heavy it stopped the dragging by six each evening. And after two hours of travelling this afternoon they might have to tie up for smoke and darkness, for no searchlight could find the shoreline. The new boats that were running them off the river had radar and depth-sounders; the boats that wouldn't touch this last shipment of the season. But McAlpine was ready to risk the down-river run rather than wait for rain or a change of wind, or even for morning — all the sandbars in the Mackenzie be damned.

The boat had backed around in a half-circle and now pointed downstream and northward. Peter rang both engines to stop, and immediately on the decks below him the mate had

17

the deckhands running; they began to drop *301* forward to be lashed solid in front of *309*. Peter stepped to the counter along the back of the pilothouse and wrote in the logbook:

> 1410 hrs: loading completed and hooking up barges to depart Norman Wells. Pushing *309* and *301*. Heavy smoke cover from forest fire. Barometer falling.

Then he selected two rolled charts from the rack over the counter and held each open for a moment before letting it coil itself into two rolls of paper. The first showed the track from Norman to the Hume River. He had pencilled corrections of his own onto the old yellow chart, especially below Ogilvie Island. The second showed the Sans Sault Rapids in detail; a pattern of soundings from where Mountain River enters the Mackenzie to the last rapids at the foot of the Dummit Islands. They would be approaching the Sans Sault in darkness; satisfied, he put down the charts and returned to the open window and leaned through. Jerry Pottle signalled that they were ready to start at slow ahead. Peter rang the engine-room.

And now he was glad the skipper had insisted they depart, for they were running again. Leaving that tiny blotch of civilization and the shore people and Kettle Fraser behind.

Running was the essence. Boat and river and sky and a thin line of earth and around every bend another bend. All held in delicate and fluid balance by the pilot. He alone knew where to go; his eyes, his hands, were pitted against the deceptively bland surface of the water. He guided the crew and the cargo. From a point to a clump of spruce, from a rock to a cutbank, from a ripple to the outside of a grey streak to a lone tree. These were his secrets: where and when to take a channel up the outside of Saline Island that would save four hours of running-time, when to make a crossing below Head of the Line that would save three miles. Watching the wash for indications of shoal water, feeling the boat suck down over a bar and knowing and remembering where to travel on the upriver trip. Eleven hundred miles of river in his head; but they were a different eleven hundred miles in spring or fall, in rising or falling water, morning or evening, wind or calm. A man at the wheel and a man in the engine-room. Joined by an indicator hand and the jingle of bells. They did not have to hear each other's voices. Here the pilot's eyes and hands were in isolated yet absolute command. Pure. He wanted to shout the word. This is mine. Storm, ice, wind, rock — those can challenge me. But here a man is defined free from the terrors of human relationships. A man's function is so clear that each is simply called chief, skipper, second, pilot. And in a few minutes they'll be settled down again: the deckhands sleeping and standing watch and scrubbing and painting and waking the next shift and sleeping again; the skipper and the first pilot asleep in the lazy afternoon, the cook up from the galley to take a short nap before supper, the second in the din of the engine-room reading a frayed and greasy magazine he has read twice before, the mate dawdling over a cup of coffee in the galley, his only worry a fresh cake the cook thinks is hidden, and should or shouldn't he dare cut himself a piece. Six on and six off neatly portioning the day, the absolute responsibility of the wheel and the fine irresponsibility of a private cabin, with a few books to read, clothes to wash, sleep to be got in preparation for the next watch. No confusion about who is to do what and who did what. From bunk to galley to the wheelhouse again, six hours on, six hours off, and always out beyond the wheelhouse the thin band of shoreline and trees, separating water and sky. An order maintained as precariously as that maintained by the hands on the wheel. The chaos held in check . . .

Except that now Hornyak gives it all another meaning. The running had long been a running away — from land, from people, from the confusion of loading and unloading, from checking the mail, from picking up waybills and dipping shore tanks and sealing barge compartments; from finding powdered milk and fruit juice and toilet paper and soap and potatoes and carrots and fresh meat to satisfy eleven people: a running away from the settlements scattered every hundred and fifty miles along the river, with their promise of booze and fights and lonely women. From home.

But must he now run away from the river too —

Pottle was signalling; he whistled, two fingers held to his teeth. The barges were in line, the pushing posts on the stern of the lead barge set against the square bow of the second barge, the square stern of the second barge set tight against the worn and splintered old pushing posts on the squared-off bow of the boat. From the high wheelhouse Peter could look out in all directions. The deckhands were bent over, working rapidly, tightening the steel wires with ratchets that clicked and paused, clicked and paused. Holding the wheel steady with one hand, he reached back to the telegraph and rang for full ahead on both engines. He glanced back past the stack, past the lifeboat and the tow winch and the little tin chimney of the galley with its coolie hat turning in the wind, and as a tremor ran through the boat he saw the water churn white at the stern.

To the starboard Norman Wells was a dim outline of silver-coloured oil-tanks set in a neat row on the bank. The forest and the low, worn Franklin Mountains behind the camp were gone from sight in the blue-grey smoke. The port-side shoreline was invisible; even Bear and Goose islands in their bright autumn foliage were not to be seen. Pottle was already coming back along the wall of stacked and tarpaulined deck-freight, checking the lashings.

The forward barge was showing little more than a foot of freeboard. It was drawing six feet of water and they couldn't be sure of a six-foot channel in the Sans Sault Rapids. The skipper, who always took the boat out or landed, had said he was too tired to see and was gone to his cabin for an hour's rest. He had been up day and night pushing the cleaning and loading operations, just as Peter had been busy on the river. For three days he was hardly out of a small boat — to avoid Kettle, he told himself. But today when he saw her plane take off he found he must still go on searching. He found himself wanting to find the body almost as badly as he wanted it to be gone forever. And the moment of his own departure seemed now not to have brought the relief he had promised himself through all those hours in a boat by himself, stiff and cramped and hunched, holding a line and grappling-hooks with one hand and steering with the other, running after dark when the others had quit.

Running and searching. That was it. He was searching too; even as he fled. Always looking for something. Three days of searching. Six years. Now he could admit to himself, he had guessed Hornyak was in the galley when he went down there for dinner; he knew Hornyak was there, waiting and watching; he knew and went down the three steps into the galley and saw the cook bent over her stove, the Eskimo eating soup, the dark, gaunt man at the head of the table, waiting, straightening his tie with a gesture that was half a twitch:

'Hello,' surprised and not surprised, came to Peter's lips; and then he stepped over the chipped green bench and sat down with the Eskimo boy between him and Hornyak. Hornyak picked up his knife and fork and didn't answer or offer a handshake. He was wearing a clean white shirt and an English tie, but the stubble of beard on his gaunt dark face made him look restless, too intent; as if he might eat his empty plate. 'Pass the spuds, Guy.' He pointed jerkily with his knife.

The dish was still warm and the whipped potatoes showed spots of warm melted butter and a trace of pepper; Peter turned up the plate that was upside down on the linoleum-covered table before him, and as he helped himself before handing the bowl to the Eskimo boy who was waiting with one hand raised Hornyak continued: 'Well, Guy, I was beginning to think I'd have to buy this whole North country to find you.'

But he laughed. No engines were running and the laugh echoed on the steel bulkheads in the silent close galley. The blower that fed air and oil into the cook-stove was humming, and after Hornyak stopped laughing Peter could hear it again.

21

'You find your human sacrifices, don't you?' Peter said.

'I've been sitting at the head of this table for three meals' (through a mouthful of potatoes now) 'and in three meals I haven't seen the skipper or mate or the chief engineer, and only one man sober enough to pass for a deckhand.'

'They'll be here when the barges are loaded. Pass the gravy.'

'But the goddamned barges won't be loaded until somebody cleans them out so Imperial Oil will load them. They told me that by radio two days ago.'

'I'm just second pilot.'

'You've got two hands.'

'I get paid because I've got a river in my head.'

'A white river bum with a river for a head.' Hornyak cut a huge steak in half on the meat plate. 'And I didn't buy this boat to turn it into a goddamned beer-parlour.'

Peter stirred his high-topped boots under the table. Hornyak, in a tramp's clothing, could make anyone else feel indecently dressed. And now he was straightening that tie again. 'Into a goddamned fish bin.'

The cook handed Peter the gravy. She was thirty-six or thirty-seven, fond of her own cooking, but not so unattractive that a man alone with her on a riverboat and a week's travel from Fort Smith or Hay River or Yellowknife mightn't knock on her door one night to ask if she wanted a drink. 'You boys can swear your souls into hell when you're out –'

'And you,' through more potatoes. 'This isn't a whorehouse either. You'd better start pretending you're a lady.'

The Eskimo boy bent to his plate, his glossy black hair dropping over his eyes and smelling sweetly of hair oil.

The cook banged down a dish of creamed carrots. 'Mister, you can't beg borrow or steal another cook short of five hundred miles. And I ain't too anxious to winter in Tuktuk.'

'And my wife will be here by two o'clock – if this young man' – indicating the Eskimo deckhand – 'can drive a jeep out to the airstrip and back. And meantime where can I find an extension cord and a light and an air-pump and a bucket?'

'They should be under lock and key,' Peter said, 'and I'm not the chief or the mate or the skipper.' He helped himself to the half of a steak that Hornyak had left and he tried to eat in silence. But Hornyak spoke again:

'How long you been on these boats?'

'You know how long.'

'Ever since —'

Peter glanced up from slicing his meat, his hand tightening on the knife, and Hornyak was smiling, his perfect teeth bright in his dark, intense face, the face just a little haggard behind the intensity. Peter noticed now there was a small purple bruise on the side of Hornyak's chin.

Hornyak gestured with his fork and knife: 'Why didn't you come looking for me, Guy? You must have heard I was in camp.'

'Go f—' But he checked himself.

'I was hoping last night to find you. Thought you might know some pretty girls.'

'I'm not a pimp.'

'Thought you might want to fix up a buddy. Before my old lady flew in.'

'I'll get you a pump and light. Just hold your horses. And let me eat.'

'You ought to be a big eater, Guy. A big man like you. Won't you have seconds of something?'

'I should go outside and throw up.'

'Guy, you're finicky. You've got no principles. You ought to get killing mad, Guy. Personal pride and all that. Family honour. A man from a good family like you. You got two hands.' Hornyak gestured once more with his knife. 'I'll do this job myself while the rest of you think about it.'

'I said, I'll get you a pump and a light.'

Pottle came up the ladder in front of the pilot-house and around to a door and entered. Pottle, underfed-looking, though he was forever going to the galley to prepare himself a huge snack; skinny Pottle who considered an accumulation of one thousand dollars sufficient reason to retire immediately, and who daily imagined a world in which the reality of his inevitable extravagance made him truly a prince to the ladies, a king to men, while all the time his apparent role as joker was a private pretence. 'Some awful terrible, the smoke out there, Guy. I don't know how you see to keep this outfit off dry land.'

Peter, by way of answer, as if himself caught faking, began to take the wheel hard over to port side.

Pottle tried once more to close his worn denim jacket over his worn flannel shirt, though two of the three supposed buttons were again proving absent. 'You must like this damned water. The way you were out dragging when you should have been sporting with the widow.'

'I'm leaving that up to an old cocksman like you.'

'But I'm finished with women myself. Finished and done with women. Leaving the field to you kids. Hanging up my sword and buckler.' Pottle abandoned the attempt to close his jacket and opened it as if he'd intended all along to wear it in a dashing manner, both hands plunged deep in his pants pockets. 'Only I'd have to be blind as a bat not to notice Mrs. Hornyak. And if I didn't see her eyes following you, I'd borrow a clean shirt – '

A deckhand entered the pilot-house. 'Off one of the deckhands instead of off you,' Pottle finished. And he didn't go on.

'You borrowing money again, mate?' Billy Abraham, a squat and fat-faced half-breed who looked vaguely like a bear ready to hibernate, came in and opened a drawer and took out a worn deck of cards and a cribbage board. 'My God, he'll keep us *all* broke.'

'I'm just lending Guy here a few thousand, since he's so hard up.' Pottle, elaborately, bent and picked up two dead bulldog flies and put them elaborately into an ashtray – a reminder to the deckhand that the pilot-house needed cleaning.

Abraham pushed aside the river charts and turned around

24

and with a jump that threatened to re-order his whole fat body he sat on the counter. He began dealing a cribbage hand.

The wheelhouse was a square room painted white with three windows front and back and two windows, separated by a door, on either side. The wide counter ran along the back wall below the three windows, with a series of drawers built in beneath. On the counter lay a logbook and radio log and a pair of binoculars, along with the two river charts. A clock and a barometer were mounted between two of the rear windows. The two-way radio was mounted on the port-side wall. In front of the high wheel was a compass set just below the window, with a small red light set over it, so it could be read at night when they were crossing Great Slave Lake with all lights out in the pilot-house. Beside the wheel was a high stool. Within reach of the wheel was the telegraph, and above the stool two sets of small wheels were set against the ceiling for manipulating the searchlights on the pilot-house roof. A cord with an iron ring on the end led to the boat's whistle.

Abraham broke two wooden matches in half and set up the four halves as cribbage pegs. 'You know where we're going?' he asked suddenly to Peter.

'Who knows where we're going?' Pottle picked up one of the two hands of cards. 'With that woman aboard.'

Now it was only Peter who laughed. 'You still muttering about Angi? Christ, the skipper is always telling you about his rights – '

'I mean that Hornyak woman with the ass on her like a tame bee.'

Peter had put his head out the window, trying to follow the crest of water that broke away from the bow of the forward barge and angled toward an invisible shore. He stayed leaning out of the window, the smell of smoke in his nostrils; the smell of burning forest faint, tainting the fresh cool air as the smell of burnt flesh had tainted it three days before. Smoke in his eyes, his nostrils; smoke obscuring what he had done, what he must do. And then, trying to sound careless: 'She flew down to Aklavik this afternoon. I saw the Otter take off.'

'But not for Aklavik.' Pottle searched through a coffee-tin looking for a butt that was long enough to be worth lighting. 'For the south and dear old Yellowknife. And not with the lady aboard.'

'It's icing up so bad down at Aklavik.' Abraham wheezed a little where he sat fat and hunched on the counter. 'A float plane couldn't get in. And it'll be six weeks before you can trust the ice. So what could the skipper do when she wanted a ride?'

Peter hated the first rap of joy that surprised the back of his head. I am not pleased. Don't look at me that way. Don't wait for what I have to say. The woman means nothing to me. It's over. We're finished. I don't want to see her again. I didn't want to see that goddamned Hornyak.

Abraham banged the counter with the bottom of his fist. 'Fifteen for two.' He pegged two points on the cribbage board and Pottle pulled up the broken match with which Abraham had pegged and struck it and lit a butt. 'She's in a hurry to see her old man,' he said, returning the burnt match to the board. 'Or so she claims. If you're the kind that believes women.'

'Ain't he that big Scotchman', Abraham said, banging down another card and pegging again, 'that likes his booze? That free-trader? He stayed with the 'Skimos when the government moved the town to Inuvik.'

Pottle played and again couldn't peg. 'So she's still aboard. And with her in the cook's cabin the skipper can't get his poontang when he wants it. And that means there's going to be misery in store for all of us.'

Peter waited.

'The mate's a fine one to talk.' Abraham was counting the points in his hand. 'He'll be suffering more than the skipper. That's why he's getting so damned grouchy.'

'I'm finished and done with the creatures. They've been the curse of my mortal existence. Kept me weary and broke, they have. All my whole miserable life. You young buggers have no idea what a curse it is to be fascinating to women.'

Peter watched the blue-grey smoke before him. The sun was a red porthole in the cool gloom. He leaned far forward through the open window beside the wheel, one boot resting on a spoke, trying to get some fresh air. But the air had a faintly unhealthy smell, as of animals caught in the unchecked blaze of the wild fire.

He had led Hornyak into the engine-room and had silently let him pick up a lamp that didn't have a shield over the bulb. *And 'Forget it' he told Hornyak as they stood in the doorway of the engine-room, when Mike thanked him for finding the equipment. And the soft irony of Mike's own 'I never forget' for an instant sent hate into his hands. For he had not forgotten either, had not been able to forget that night in the mountains when he opened the door of the room where Kettle was supposedly resting, sleeping after their hike up the glacier, when he saw the image of Kettle, of the two of them, caught in a mirror; and remembering that moment, that moment that had become six years, he could have killed Hornyak; he could have hit him with a wrench or a hammer and dropped him overboard and gone crying for help, and before he could get help the current would have worked a revenge upon Michael Hornyak:* Peter, now, at the wheel and heading north, as he had been ever since that night, confessed to himself that he had had that impulse — but that was after he led Hornyak to the equipment — *after*, he told himself, *after, after —*

The skipper, at four-thirty the next morning, in long underwear and sheepskin-lined boots and a parka, came pounding on Peter's door to say the fog had lifted and the searchlights could pierce the darkness. They had dropped anchor in the middle of the channel the previous night, just above the Sans Sault Rapids. The smoke and fog were so thick they couldn't approach the riverbank. Peter unzipped himself reluctantly from his warm sleeping-bag and five minutes later found the deckhands hauling up the anchor with the hand capstan on the bow of *Barge 301*. Frost lay heavy on the steel deck where the four deckhands cursed and joked and worked in the darkness, the stacked oil-drums cutting off the glare from the searchlights. Peter looked out at the invisible pattern of rocks and current that awaited him, at the steady rush of water; then he hurried back along the edge of the two barges, past the oil-drums and the reefer and the tarpaulined deck-freight, and he climbed to the pilot-house and saw the skipper had found time to put on his trousers.

They quickly learned that all the buoys had been picked up for the winter by the government boat. But in forty-five minutes, travelling at half speed, two men tiring themselves at the wheel, they were through the white water that would mean three hours or more of nerve-wracking work for the pilots and engineers on the upstream trip; Peter turned the wheel over to Jonas at six and went down to the galley to a breakfast of hotcakes and fried eggs and bacon, and by six-thirty, before Kettle came out of the cook's cabin, he was back in his sleeping-bag.

Only to get up again at nine. By nine-fifteen they were approaching the top of the Ramparts. He wanted to look at the hump of water that would be the chief obstacle on their return. He wanted to decide what his strategy might be. The Ramparts loomed out of the smoke, a limestone wall that became a chute eight miles long. A canyon. And in the late fall a rib of Precambrian rock across the top of the entrance made a hump of water in the only deep channel. Old Jonas Bird looked at the cresting rock that edged the channel and pulled the plaid ski-cap low over his brown squinted eyes and told the skipper to rent himself a dog-team down on the coast. Or an igloo, he added. The skipper cursed and said they would

have to be back here and through in a matter of a few days
or they'd never get through. Peter looked at the slanting rush
of water and realized he had something new and frightening
to learn about the river, and he went to the galley to have a
cup of coffee before they passed Fort Good Hope.

At the little trappers' settlement a crowd of men and women
and children, mostly Indian, sprinkled here and there with a
white, gathered on the high bank to watch the boat slip past.
They gathered against the sky, coming from the red-roofed
Hudson's Bay post and the white mission buildings and the
disorderly scattering of unpainted log houses. The men, in
open embroidered blue parkas, squatted down on their haunch-
es and smoked and watched but did not raise a hand, as if to
wave would be to confess a belief in the boat's presence that
was not warranted by common sense. Two deckhands went out
on deck and waved mightily, and a group of young girls, in
colourful sweaters and dark skirts and moccasins, returned the
greeting hesitantly, taking courage from each other and gig-
gling together, their teeth flashing alive in their dark faces. A
woman with a child in a shawl on her back came down the
bank toward the beach, two sleigh dogs following, and she dip-
ped herself a pail of water and stopped among the empty canoes to watch briefly before turning back up the hill.

Peter ate early, at eleven-thirty, to avoid meeting Kettle in
the galley, and came up to take the wheel from Jonas.

Now, late in the afternoon, the skipper in turn took the
wheel. Peter stepped to the back of the pilot-house. He opened
the logbook where a stub of pencil marked the place. Finding
the lead broken he fished in his pockets for another stub, reading the last entry while he did so:

> Crossed Arctic Circle. Weather improving.
> Smoke thinning and boat making good time.
> Hurray!

It was the skipper's entry. But a second hand, recognizable as
Jonas Bird's, had added in awkward letters:

> But heading downstream at the end of Sept.
> What the hell are we doing here?

Now Peter, finding a pencil with lead, glanced around once more as if to confirm his location and made his own entry:

> 1620 hrs: Calm and clear. Hit sand bar while
> crossing toward Burnt Point. Ouch.

They were hard aground somewhere north of where the Ontaratue River flows into the Mackenzie. In flat country. In a stretch of river so wide it seemed motionless, like a broad northern lake on a windless day. McAlpine himself was bemused by a quiet sense of disbelief. He cut off both engines and stared quietly at the forward barge, at the unbroken mirror of water surrounding the bow, unwilling to believe that a few minutes earlier he had been awakened by a hesitation so subtle yet powerful, on the boat's part, that it sent his head gently nudging the forward rail of his bunk. In a little over a day's travel he had gained four hours on their anticipated running-time; he was unwilling to acknowledge a delay.

A thin veil of smoke diffused the light in the cloudless sky. Only a wavering line of darker blue separated the pale sky from water of the same indifferent colour. Illusion and reality were confounded in a softly shining landscape, the sky upset into its own reflection.

McAlpine began to pull on the wheel and spoke to Peter almost politely as he did so: 'Go have some coffee while the old man gets you off.'

But Peter only turned from the window on the starboard side of the wheel and picked up the binoculars and stepped to an open door. Burnt Point, with its patch of naked grey spruce trunks, stripped by a fire years earlier, was hardly visible even through the binoculars. He had begun his crossing, he now guessed, maybe thirty yards too late.

No current showed in the apparently still water, but here the crossings were treacherous, narrow, winding, subject to quick change. Off to the port side lay a series of sandbars, clean and flat, like playgrounds prepared for children who for some mysterious reason never appeared. Beyond the sandbars was a willow-covered island awash in its own reflection, fringed by a grey tangle of driftwood that had been caught on the low island. The shore itself, for all its willow and spruce and tamarack, was half water, half ponds and sloughs. But today no geese, no ducks or swans rose from the ponds and sloughs to skim the half-drowned trees. Six spruce, standing straight in what seemed to be a neat row on a flat island behind them, were the only objects breaking the flat horizon, and somehow they seemed taller than the sky. Man intruded only occasionally on this blur of landscape, for a few hours on a long afternoon of the brief furious season of open water. The chaos had not yet been resolved into form; men could find no cause for stopping. They did not map the shifting channels; they did not count the sandbars that grew like mushrooms in the night.

The skipper let go the wheel and it spun of its own accord; he saw he had guessed the current wrong and began deliberately to swing the rudders in the other direction. 'Damn,' he said. 'Get me a cup of coffee, somebody.'

Next day, nineteen hours later, the water was still calm, the sky was calm, the air was calm. And the skipper was in a rage. He called Peter and the mate and all the deckhands a pack of constipated dry-land peckerheads who didn't know their arses from a punchboard or a hayrake from a bottle of whisky, and he told the cook to go take a flying run at the moon when she told him to watch his language at her galley table. He tried backing off the sandbar. Then he tried to jerk the barge free, slacking off on a tow-line, getting up speed and hitting the end of the line like a calf on a rope. He spilled the cook's pancake dough all over the galley and knocked a loafing deckhand off the toilet stool: but didn't budge the barge. 'We'll be caught in a damned sandstorm if we don't get off here by dawn,' he said. He kept the crew up all night and very nearly bent a

31

prop manoeuvring in the darkness, trying to swing the barge back and forth to work it afloat. In the middle of the morning he finally hooked onto the marooned barge and rang both engines to full astern and told the engineers to turn on both superchargers, and he sat down to wait for the wash from the two screws to dig a channel in which the barge could drift free. The pilot-house windows rattled in their frames. But no one dared speak.

Peter finally found an excuse that would get him outside; he went onto the stuck barge to tie a sounding-pole upright to the capstan, so the man at the wheel, lining up with something beyond the pole, could see if there was any movement. He almost stepped on Kettle where she sat in the late morning sun, half asleep in the queer light; he started back as if he had nearly stepped overboard.

The sky had cleared of smoke; it was a bright and strangely warm day. So warm the world seemed to be coming to pieces. The horizon bumped in one place; in another it trailed off into the sky as if unravelling.

The stack of oil-drums hid the two of them from the pilot-house. Peter, after he put up the red and white sounding pole, instead of going back to the boat sat down on the capstan head.

Kettle was dressed in slacks and a loose pullover sweater; she was propped against a coil of tow-line, her face into the sun and her eyes closed. The low V in the neck of the man's sweater showed where her suntan ended, and Peter watched the sun on her soft flesh; then she turned her head away, not speaking, and the light caught a pearl in an ear-ring.

He waited, poised like a runner against the capstan. In the silence he heard the sand scraping the sides of the barge, blasted along by the propellers. He wanted to speak of her father, to warn her, perhaps. To remind her. He touched his tongue to his dry lips.

He could not speak now, yet on his first downriver trip, as a deckhand, he had gone eagerly to see Kettle's father and had met a rough hard-drinking man who lived with an Eskimo woman. A huge man who told Peter off-handedly that his wife died when Kettle was born; the Eskimo woman raised her. Fifteen years ago he had gone out to civilization for a month's holiday and in ten days had returned north. The outside was suffocating, he said. But it represented all he wanted his daughter to have. He sent her out as a child to a nuns' school in Winnipeg, though she wasn't Catholic, and then to an eastern university. He wanted his daughter to remember nothing. And when Peter met her in university the wilderness she had been exiled from was a forbidden land, yet a world to which she dreamed of returning, for it had become freedom and excitement and utopia to her. But her father didn't even want her to come home for her summer holidays, and he was pleased to hear she was working that summer in a mountain resort, for there she would do the right things and meet the right people.

Peter, after his first visit, never went to see the trader again. But he kept an ear open to the gossip that passed up and down the river; the chatter of idle men when boats tied up beside each other at Norman Wells or in Yellowknife. Gordon Fraser always had a scheme for making a million. He went on trading flour and sugar and tea for muskrat skins and white fox skins. He gave supplies to families that would never pay him, because when they had furs to sell they went to someone else. But when he met men from the outside he had schemes to unfold. He wanted to ship arctic char to the outside, as a delicacy. That was his latest scheme. And before that, talking to anyone who would listen, he wanted to buy up all the small fishing outfits on Great Slave Lake. Peter listened to the gossip, and he knew that Kettle had not been home in six years.

Now he had been up all night and was half asleep, like the day itself. The sun was warm on the back of his neck. Hornyak had jumped from the bow of this barge, presumably in an attempt to put out the flames of his burning clothing. Peter glanced away from the glare of sun off the water to Kettle and realized suddenly that she was not out here simply to be warm. She too had memories. Her six years of the past. Nights when he was on the riverboat, watching water and shore. Where was she all those nights? Those times when he lay in his bunk and listened and heard only the monotony of two engines pushing him through the hours. She had a memory he could never know, never share. Another six years could not recall it. He awakened abruptly to his own jealousy. And to a thought that was worse: perhaps he had wanted Hornyak to take her. But no. Their innocence had been enough for both of them. At university. If he was going into law he'd be a student for years. They'd agreed on that. He had little money. It was best not to start anything. All his common sense told him that. All his background told him that. He was from a good family, if not from a wealthy one. And if a harsh longing sometimes disagreed, that was only natural too: he had not wanted to find Hornyak there. They were friends. He trusted a friend with secrets —

Kettle glanced up and caught him staring and her eyes were for an instant warm: 'What did you do on that trip?' she asked.

'That trip?'

'Across the prairies. When you were coming to the mountains. That time — '

'What did I do?'

'Peter, he told me. I said you were so good. He really — instead of defending myself I said you were good, and he laughed that confident laugh and said ask him about that girl we picked up in Regina.'

Peter shook his head.

'Then you didn't?'

'I took my turns.'

'Afterwards — I was afraid. What if he'd lied?'

Peter shook his head again. 'He never really lied, you know. He was so goddamned honest in ways. That's what disarmed people. With women — like when he wanted a woman he just told her. And so often' — he slid down off the capstan head and sat hunched against it — 'on the prairies — it was hot, and a bone-dry spring. Dusty. And we'd walk into those little Chinese restaurants or beer-parlours in the little towns, and pretty soon women would come up to our table, as if some great bloody redeemer had walked into the room. And he'd redeem them all right. Against a wall or in the back seat of a car or out in somebody's back yard on the grass. He redeemed them so well that one time he was so sore he kept himself wrapped in cotton batting for two days. And we would drive.'

'But don't you see.' Kettle sat up, leaned forward. 'He wasn't faithful to me for a month of his life. He wasn't faithful to anything. Your great shining ideal was a plain ordinary son of a bitch.'

'He wasn't my ideal at all. He scared me to death. And why are you sitting out here,' Peter said, 'at the shrine of the martyr?'

She gave a cry of surprise. 'Peter, you're wrong.' She started to reach out to touch him, then stopped. 'But why, Peter, for God's sake, why didn't you phone or write or something when you were missing for those nine days?'

He gestured out at the water, at the mirage that unravelled the horizon. 'One day — out there on the prairies in a small farmers' town — I sat down and filled out a postcard. Mike was sleeping off the night before in the car and I was having coffee. And then the message ran on so I bought another card, and then I needed another; and all this little café had was cards with pictures on them of rabbits as big as horses and potatoes four or five to a wagon-load. And pretty soon I had thirteen cards covered.'

'But I didn't get them.'

'I only had stamps for a few. Four or five, maybe.'

'But I didn't get any, Pete. Never. None.'

'I don't believe I mailed them.' He slapped the pockets of his denim pants as if he might still have them somewhere. 'Maybe I left them in the café.'

'But can't you at least tell me what you said?'

'No.' He paused, kicked at the loose end of a line, then shrugged. 'Look, I remember exactly what I said.' He shook his head once and violently. 'I said Kettle, I've met him – the kind of man you should be marrying. So help me God. This is what you deserve, I said. But then I got it all down on thirteen cards and I couldn't send them. None of them. I threw them all in a garbage can. A couple of days later, in another town. I carried them around – three days it was. But Kettle – '

'Listen,' she said.

A new sound came to their ears. Not the sound of sand grating along the steel sides of the barge but a harsher sound, low at first, then rising in pitch, from the barge's bottom. Tons of grinding steel on pebbles. Kettle jumped to her feet. 'Listen!'

'Good,' he said. 'We're moving.'

'Listen, for God's sake!'

'But Kettle, I know I should have sent word. You've got to see why I couldn't write – '

'Listen,' she was crying. 'Just listen, Pete! That noise!'

'Be careful!' he said.

'From under the water,' she shouted. 'Like a scream!'

'No!' he said.

'Like a scream!' She leaped away.

'No!' he shouted.

Recklessly, she raced along the edge of the barge, back toward the boat.

He went to the bow and looked down at the water; he could see only a muddied swirl. 'No,' he said to no one. He turned away and Kettle had disappeared behind the big reefer. 'No,' he insisted one time more.

Aklavik. An Eskimo word. The place

of the brown bear. A trapping settlement in the Mackenzie delta; in a maze and tangle of channels that confound all but the best pilots; in an epidemic of ponds and lakes and marshes. After two days the *Nahanni Jane* arrived here from the crossing at Burnt Point. The willows in the delta were bare of all leaves. The poplars were bare. The country was already still, freezing into winter. The first day of no sun was fast approaching. And the boat was 175 miles from Tuktoyaktuk out on the coast; the crew still had deck-freight and oil to deliver – or the tiny port and its new airstrip would run out of fuel-oil and supplies before the drift-ice moved next July. And from listening in on other radio skeds McAlpine knew that in twenty-four hours his would be the last crew left on the river below The Wells.

Jonas Bird was at the wheel when they landed in Aklavik, although it was early afternoon. The skipper had scornfully told him to stand Peter's watch while they were in the forty miles of the narrow and winding and often silted Aklavik Channel. So Peter was on the bow of the lead barge with the deck-hands as it smashed its way through the ice toward shore.

An arctic raven caught his eye when it hopped out from behind a willow clump, dragging a rotten jackfish that even the sleigh-dogs had ignored. The raven protested hoarsely and hopped again, then with one more awkward hop it took off and flapped away, the gritty intestine trailing from its beak. A man appeared on the beach, another followed him; and the shore-line came alive.

Johnny Louttit gathered half the coils of the heaving line in each hand. The ball of rope on the end of the line twirled once over his head; then he flung it along with the coils in his right hand and the line snaked out of his left hand; then the line in the air – it too snaked out of its flying coil and the ball bounced on the transparent ice and skidded ashore. An Eskimo man, small in his big parka, picked up the end and began to pull. Louttit quickly tied his end of the heaving line to the loop of the headline. The Eskimo pulled the heavy head-line ashore, getting help now from others, and he pushed the loop of line through the eye of a deadman and shoved a block of wood into the loop. On deck young Abraham, quick for all his fatness, took three turns on the capstan and began to pull the line tight.

A crowd was collecting on the bank of frozen mud; word was spreading that a boat was in. The sudden freeze had caught a dozen schooners and mud scows tied up to shore. Two float planes, Beavers, were anchored and locked in the ice in the Peel Channel. Men in brightly trimmed parkas came quickly down to the beach; groups of children edged up more carefully to join the men, here and there a child finding a man's hand inside a long, fur-edged sleeve. Women in twos and threes stood farther back, ducking out from the wooden shacks and scows and tents along the shore; they checked their dark hair, watched shyly, the fur trim showing on the hoods and cuffs and bottoms of their calf-length dresses, the decorations bright on their mukluks.

In a few minutes the boat was in to shore and a deckhand pushed out a gangplank, a single cleated two-by-six that bowed with a man's weight. Peter went back to the boat to help Kettle with her luggage.

'I don't see anybody who looks like your father.'

'I imagine he expected me yesterday.'

Kettle was wearing a tight-fitting blue suit. She was already struggling to get her bags down from the bow of the boat onto the heavily loaded barge. Peter lowered her bags onto the barge and reached up and guided her feet as she searched for the two steel steps welded on the outside of the bow. She stepped down as he helped and his hand brushed the inside of her leg. He said nothing and she pretended not to have noticed.

'Are you busy, Pete?'

'I'm supposed to be on duty. And the skipper is up there in the pilot-house looking for an excuse to fire my ass off this boat.' He picked up her two large suitcases and nodded toward the narrow passage between the deck-freight and the edge of the barge. 'So let's hurry — and watch the bollards.' He started and she followed behind carrying her small suitcase. They hurried down the gangplank, where seven or eight men were being signed on by the mate to help the deckhands roll drums of oil ashore. Two deckhands, the white boy and Louttit, were beginning to knock over drums of oil with a bang that sent them bouncing on the steel deck. Abraham was setting up a gangplank so he could roll the drums off the top row.

Peter glanced back at the two barges and the boat; the pilot-house was empty; the cook, standing at the rail in front of her open cabin door, waved as if he were leaving, not Kettle. He led the way up the bank. Jimmie Kartuk was talking to three young Eskimoes in ducktail haircuts and cowboy boots. They were speaking of a dance when a closed-in jeep roared up beside them. But Gordon Fraser wasn't in it; Peter recognized the bearded driver as a bush pilot.

The wooden sidewalk took them away from the shore. In a few minutes Kettle led the way into a small store that smelled of Indian-tanned moosehide. It was dimly lit and crammed to the ceiling with shelves and boxes of canned foods, with sacks and crates and gun-racks and rolled tents and sleeping-bags and boots and clothes and hardware and drugstore items: a winter's supply.

'Can I help you?' a Loucheux girl asked from behind a candy-covered counter; the shield on her blue blazer was that of the new Sir Alexander Mackenzie school in Inuvik.

'Is dad here?'

'Is — '

Peter interrupted: 'We're looking for Mr. Fraser.'

'Oh.' The girl pointed a bright red fingernail and began to explain; before she had finished Kettle was turning away and leading Peter toward the door. They walked between the wall of the store and a boarded-up hotel: at the door of the house she forgot to knock.

Gordon Fraser looked up from where he was teasing a Husky pup. He seemed puzzled at the sight of people in the doorway; but he lifted a fur cap off his huge head and revealed a great woolly mop of uncombed grey hair that looked as if he was wearing a second cap under the first. He rose clumsily. He was wearing a red plaid shirt that was now too large for his once huge body, a pair of black woollen trousers that had apparently never been ironed, and mukluks and moccasin rubbers. His large brown face and hawk nose came at the door, still not a hint of recognition flickering into his pale blue eyes. The smell of dog and whisky preceded him. 'He was a good man – in his own way.'

Then he saw Kettle's confusion. 'You should have told me. The Hudson's Bay man heard it on his short-wave.' He motioned them into the room. 'He listens to the boats talking. For something to do.'

The house itself was as neat as the man was unkempt. The Eskimo woman, wearing white tennis shoes and a simple blue cotton dress and a white sweater, her hair in a neat black braid, was much younger than Fraser. She was small and quiet, and quietly, noiselessly, she crossed the room from the kitchen door. She embraced Kettle gently, the two women embracing, Kettle tall over the other woman; and Peter, awkward at the door, heard the Eskimo woman say in her soft gentle accent, 'I'm sorry for you.' And awkwardly he and Fraser shook hands, muttering, Fraser not letting on if he didn't remember Peter, his grip like iron.

Fraser had aged many years since Peter had last seen him. He walked slowly and sat down slowly into an easy chair covered with an imitation Indian blanket and picked up a drink off an end-table that held two pictures in gilt frames; Kettle as a small girl in long dark curls and holding a teddy bear, a snapshot blown up; and a posed picture of an older and very beautiful woman who must have been Kettle's mother. He smiled at Kettle when she turned away from the Eskimo woman. But then he said, 'It was a terrible accident. Terrible. But things like that can't be helped – ' He could find no words and took a drink.

Kettle, still without speaking, rushed to move her bags from where Peter had set them down in the doorway.

'Let me,' Peter said anxiously, as if there was somewhere a train to be caught in a matter of seconds. She let him take the two bags and pointed to a door next to the kitchen door. Then she ran ahead and opened it and stepped into a child's room complete with a row of children's books on a shelf over the bed, two worn lions leaning against the headboard, a doll's crib and a doll on the floor beside the bed. He could see little else in the light that came from the living-room, for a shutter was closed on the bedroom window. Only when Kettle followed him in and dropped her small suitcase on the bed did he realize the room was hers; the room of her childhood kept as it must have been before she was sent away to school.

'The skipper might be looking for me,' Peter said. He moved again to the door by which he had entered the house; but the Eskimo woman came softly across the room and caught his arm. 'Later,' she said. 'After a while, come back.' She gestured into the kitchen. 'For supper. A lot of fresh meat should be on the boat.'

Kettle collapsed onto her father's lap, spilling some of his drink.

And then Peter was standing outside, alone, aware that he could walk away and send a deckhand with a note saying he couldn't make it for supper; and by morning and the first light he would never have to see Caroline Hornyak *née* Fraser again. Never. Never, he told himself. Never. If he so chose.

He had not written his own father for a year and a half. A year ago last winter. Just after Christmas. Each time he tried he found he had less and less to talk about; each attempt showed him to be more isolated from the promises and hopes of his childhood. His family's ambitions. But now he went back to the boat and sat down on his bunk with his suitcase on his lap and he laid out a warped writing-tablet on a flat side of the suitcase.

Soon after he sat down the skipper took the boat out to break ice to release the schooners and scows and planes that had been caught in the freeze; every so often, as the charging boat hit the ice, the suitcase slid on his lap. Sometimes the boat's bow had to ride up on the ice to break it, and as it crashed through he would grab at the mattress or reach back

41

and brace himself against the bare wall.

His father was an unsuccessful lawyer in Guelph, Ontario. He was a lonely man who couldn't quite bring himself to spend his talent finding loopholes in the law; he dreamed, and it was the mother who saved pennies and came through with a handful of small bills to buy things. But not the things the father wanted for his son. The mother had wanted him to have a B.A. from the university where, she was pleased to say, she earned her own B.A. The father meditated in an ashtray-less parlour and thought his son should have a crack at owning a sports car. And a year off from school to read the classics. And maybe one of those summers digging for odds and ends in Greece or Egypt.

Peter's earliest memory was of his father in an old green Graham-Paige, a touring car almost as long as a boxcar with yellowed isinglass windows and a windshield that he would let the boy tip down so the wind would bring tears to their eyes. Unless he put on the old goggles that his father wore around his neck. And there was a worn spare tire on either side of the carefully waxed body, and the cracked leather seats were religiously cleaned. The boy and his father and a Great Dane — all together in the front seat they would explore the dusty country roads, and sometimes the father left them outside an old brick or stone hotel while he went in for a beer, and people would gather to look at the car and the dog and the boy.

And he remembered his father's dilemma; he would speed in the car, yet it was so heavy that when it was moving fast the brakes weren't strong enough to stop it; it rolled and the driver had to wait until it quit. His father delighted in the speed, yet was tortured by the immorality of steering a car that was in fact out of control. He would look for long stretches of empty road, and one time they just beat a Mennonite family's buggy to a narrow bridge.

'I was wondering,' Peter wrote, 'about that expression — an act of God. When is an accident an act of God, if it ever is, and when —'

The boat hit ice and he lost his balance and the pen dashed a line through the letter. A moment later the engines went off. Peter stood up and looked out of his cabin window. They were thirty yards from shore, trying to make a channel so the two float planes could be pulled up on the beach. As he was sitting down again the engines started.

He was turning the scratched letter into something to say to his father when a knock came at his door. He saw a deck-hand's head outside the window and heard him say, 'This is it.'

Gordon Fraser answered the invitation to enter; he stepped too high over the raised sill and turned around slowly; he closed the door with great deliberation, but the door wasn't shut when he tried it and he gave it a slam.

'How the hell did you get here?' Peter slid his suitcase onto the pillow he used with his sleeping-bag and stood up again.

'I came across the ice out there, with that maniac of a skip-per of yours trying to bust it out from under me.'

'You lead a charmed life.'

'That isn't what the skipper said. Like a damned hornet.'

Fraser brushed an army-surplus parka off the only stool in the cabin and sat down, or let himself collapse. 'You got a drink?'

'Maybe a swallow each.' Peter opened a drawer under his bunk and dug out a forty-ounce overproof Lemon Hart rum bottle. He held it up toward the window. There was three in-ches of rum over the dimple in the bottom. He kicked the draw-er shut and picked two rather dirty tumblers off the shelf over his bunk and poured two stiff drinks. 'This should take care of any germs.'

Fraser sat awkwardly on the stool and accepted the tumbler but didn't take a drink. 'What does she want?' he said.

Peter sat down and swirled the dark rum in his glass, watch-ing it. 'What does anybody want?'

'Come off the shit, Mr. Guy. Look. I gave her an education. Caroline. I sent her outside, away from all this. I brought her up to be a lady. And goddamnit she won't even let me get drunk in peace.'

'You want some water?'

'I want some peace. Ever since that girl was born, I've been trying to do the right thing. But now I just want to be left alone to mind my own business.'

'Good grief, man.' Peter took a sip of the overproof rum and coughed. 'It's her home too.'

'And it's *my* home. It's the only goddamned excuse I've got for a home. And she married that crazy bohunk or Polack or whatever he is, and she's got more money than she can spend. Now that he's swindled enough fishermen out of their boats and nets. And the crazy bastard is dead and it's all hers. She says it's all hers. She told me. And still she wants to come back and torment her old man.'

'She tries not to — '

'But she just walks in and sits there and *reminds* me, goddamnit — ' He coughed violently and now he took a drink. 'She reminds me. Don't you see that, Guy?' He bobbed his head forward. 'Guy, that's a pea-soup name.'

'A lot of people say so.'

'Well, is it or isn't it?'

'The family came from England, strangely enough. Way back. The name used to embarrass my mother no end.'

'I never liked the English.' Fraser shifted his fur cap on his head. 'I sailed alone the first time. Out of Liverpool.' He was silent, staring into his glass. Then he went on: 'Her ma didn't want me to come here to begin with. You know what I mean? And now I hate it. And I can't leave. You know what I mean, Guy? But at least I can stand it when that girl stays away.'

He swayed forward on the stool and looked straight at Peter. 'What're you doing up here, Guy? You came to my store, five years ago. Six years ago. With a lot of damned moon-faced bellywash about knowing my daughter. You're a young buck. You got everything to do yet. You going to be a riverman all your life?'

44

'I like it okay. It's a good life.'

'What's so goddamned good about it?'

'I got time to myself.'

'And what's so good about time?'

'I don't know. Something's good about it.'

'You're out of your screwing head.'

'Okay, I'm out of my screwing head.'

'Put her there, Guy.' He shook Peter's hand. 'So am I. I'm right out of my screwing head. And what am I going to do about it? I'm going to send that girl to hell out of here. And I'm going to send her out on this boat. Because if I don't she'll be here for six weeks until the ice gets hard enough so I can hire a bush pilot to take her out. And in six weeks it'll be me going out – in a strait-jacket. So she's going right now. Instead. On this boat. And that's why I walked that broken ice. So you can take her out.'

'We'll have to take *her* out in a strait-jacket.'

'You brought her here. You get her out.'

'But she came to visit you. She didn't have to come here. She *wants* – '

'It doesn't matter right now what she wants. I can't let it matter.'

'She's got a mind of her own. You ought to know that by now, Mr. Fraser.'

'And I've got a mind of my own. I came to this goddamned country because *I* wanted to come. And if I want her to leave – she'll leave.' He finished his drink with one long swallow and turned the tumbler over and watched it drip. 'It must be time for supper,' he said.

'It's getting there,' Peter said.

'I said I'd be back by supper.'

'Then it's time.'

'Come on over and eat. My wife' – he corrected himself – 'my woman made some kind of stew that's better than anything you ever ate.'

'Maybe I ought to finish my letter.'

'You've got an invitation to supper. And you're going to do me a favour.'

'But you haven't told me why she shouldn't come see – '

'Because I'm no good. I'm what you call a squaw-man. I'm a two-bit trader. I'm a drunk.'

'And you're lying,' Peter said.

Fraser lowered his voice as if to confide a secret. But his voice came loudly hoarse. 'And I killed her mother. In my own fool way. Can't you guess that, Guy? She wanted to be in Scotland with her hundreds of damned relatives. And I brought her into this goddamned godforsaken country because the Hudson's Bay could buy young Scots cheap to do their adding and subtracting. And it killed her.'

Peter offered him the little rum remaining in the bottle and he shook his head.

'The only decent thing I ever did in my life was saving enough money to get that child out of this place.'

'So you sent her out with a bank-book.'

Fraser lay down his empty glass on the bunk and stood up facing Peter, bent to him as if to convince by the power and horror of one last argument; then he put his hands on Peter's neck, Peter couldn't guess whether to caress or to strangle him. 'You dumb young bastard, Guy. A man is free here. You ever hear the word? He is so free that nothing else in the world is ever as good again. Never. But it's a screwing jail, this place. I *can't* leave. Just the sight of one skyscraper or one traffic light or one telephone booth – and I'd be back. I tried it once, Guy.'

'We got here, Mr. Fraser. And a hell of a lot of people turned out to meet the boat.'

'I wasn't there, Guy. And you got here on a river. On a river that's frozen most of the time. It's frozen hard. And I'm a free man down here, because you and your bunch can't get at me.' He laughed aloud and tightened his grip and Peter caught at the powerful wrists. 'Come on, boy. Forget about your letter. Never let anything come between you and a meal.' He let go of Peter's neck. 'There's some wild duck in this. And you never tasted anything so good in your life.'

Peter rubbed at his neck where Fraser's fingers had bruised the flesh. 'I'll see you get ashore without drowning yourself.'

Out on deck the four deckhands were shouting and cheering and stripping off their dirty work clothes in the cold air. 'That bush pilot gave us a bottle.' Louttit pushed the open bottle at Fraser, who accepted and raised it to his lips. 'That old son of a bee of a skipper,' Abraham said. 'Hired a pile of Huskies to roll barrels and gave us the night off. Last fling till Yellowknife.' He gave a hoot and began to shadow-box.

'Going dancing I'll bet,' Fraser said. 'You young bucks love to kick up your heels.'

Mud, the white deckhand, nodded vigorously. 'There's a drum dance. In that old boarded-up hotel.'

'And we're going to get Mud to try some dancing.' Jimmie Kartuk winked and flung his shirt down the shaft that led to the crew's quarters in the forecastle.

'And we'll get him fixed up,' Abraham added.

Mud's nickname reflected his ability to look dirty from head to foot even when he hadn't been on land for a week. At seventeen, his great burden in life was his virginity, and in the course of the summer his fellow deckhands, in spite of infinite promises and oaths, hadn't been able to find a remedy. A whore in Yellowknife bought him a coke and sent him back to the docks. A woman in Fort Smith sent him down to the boat to send up the skipper. Even the cook treated his boyhood as something inviolate.

'If we can't get him a girl,' Louttit promised, 'we're going to catch him a polar bear.'

Mud blushed and scratched at his crotch.

From the door leading down to the crew's quarters came the sound of a guitar. Some of Kartuk's friends were aboard and he grinned and went down the ladder to join them, humming a cowboy song as he disappeared.

'We've got to find some more rubbers,' Abraham said. 'Mud

47

promised that the way he's loaded he'll wear two.'

Mud reached for his back pocket. 'I've been carrying one all season. It's wearing a hole in my purse.' He showed everyone the ring in the leather on the outside of his wallet and everyone sympathized.

'It'll be an empty wallet by morning,' Abraham said. 'Just for God's sake take a shower, Mud.'

The boat eased close to the stern of *Barge 309* and Louttit ran to tie up. Mud went into the washroom.

Fraser handed the bottle back to Abraham and turned to Peter. 'You coming with me, or are you going to the big dance?'

'I'm a hungry man,' Peter said.

'Then you picked the right address.'

'I'm a starving man,' Peter said.

'Then get a wiggle on, boy. Time to edge up to the table.'

'I'm famished,' Peter said. 'Like a bitch wolf with her nine eager sucklings.'

'I'll tell you a secret.' Fraser stopped with one leg over the forward rail, one hand on the bitt. 'When I was arguing with my daughter — I asked about you and she said she didn't expect to see you again.' He slapped Peter hard on the shoulder. 'And I said I bet her damned awful luck she would.'

A dog wailed in the far darkness. Somewhere nearer an owl hooted. The muscles of his belly twitched once more in a motion that was now without intent. Time came back into this room, into this bed of a child, and it was not time present for Peter but the slow, seeping time of another place and another occasion; and he looked into a hotel room, started to walk in and saw them, this woman and what he thought was his best if very new friend; and in the slightly archaic splendour of that carpeted and marbled and faded room he believed he did not want to believe what he saw, the eloquence of flesh and desire caught dispassionately in the glass mirror inside the door; and even if he tried not to believe he turned and fled and kept on fleeing north and again north until he was here and a few miles from the arctic coast: he turned from the room that was to be his journey's end and found it his journey's beginning. And slept that first night, if he slept at all, on a wood-pile in the mountains. A service truck going out to the camp-sites with wood for the campers gave him his first lift and dropped him beside a wilderness track. And at dawn an elderly couple who wanted to see the sunrise picked him up stiff and cold, and they kept going north from Banff, north from Lake Louise, the old man driving on the wrong side of the road. But the sun came up as promised, splendid as blood on the jagged mountains, spilling down off the gaunt rocks to the first trees, the lakes. The old man drove on the wrong side and praised the sunrise and his wife offered candy to the bears and then to the rider she addressed as son and then to the bears again. The old man geared down into second, into low. And up they went beyond the big timber, to the white roar of streams over broken, naked rock, up and up to a great silent tongue of ice on the mountain's lip. And the old man wanted to ride a Bombardier up onto the glacier, so the passenger got out into the cool sun and the chill wind, and a pair of honeymooners picked him up; they did not speak to him or to each other, only drove on, not seeing the moose and elk, their thighs bumping because of the big stranger brooding in the front seat.

And north from the Columbia Icefields the road took a steep drop, the descent began: with a view that left them dizzy, the mountain-side of ice rubbed bright by morning, the mountain-trapped clouds gaudy with the sun. They had seen the water come new-born off the ice, after those thousands of years, and as it began its long tumble to the arctic sea they followed. They went with it. Down a long mountain trough. A new raw redness to the mountains and the smashed rock beside the new road. Leaving Sunwapta Falls, the river flat and wide and sandy green, then Athabasca Falls where it smoked through a gorge, then the river growing and flat again, sandy and green, rushing down. Down to the Arctic.

And he joined it. Followed. To a bus station. To an office

that was hiring deckhands. To an airport. To his first boat, his first season; to his second, his third. And here and now he was in a room with the woman he saw in the mirror and believed he could flee. In the room where she grew up.

And he could be indifferent now too, for the first time since then, for a moment spent and indifferent, and now he could ask the question he had wanted for so long to ask:

'Why, Kettle?'

She tipped her ear to his lips. He felt in the darkness the cool pearl in the ear-ring.

'Why did you leave that door open? Unlocked?'

She didn't speak.

'Did you know it was unlocked?'

'Yes.'

'Why?'

'I don't know why.'

'Tell me.'

'I've wondered often. He asked me to lock it. He laughed and said go lock it and I went to the door and pretended but I didn't turn the lock.'

'I don't understand. I wish I could.'

And then:

'Peter?'

'Yes?'

'Who killed him, finally?'

'I told you before. It was an accident.'

Then they were quiet for a long time and Peter couldn't bring himself to speak and listened to her breathing, not quite relaxed, and then Kettle said:

'When did they stop dancing?'

'A while ago. They were playing and they quit.'

'But they'll go till dawn. They stop for a drink or a bite to eat. Or a smoke for the drummers.' And she was remembering too. 'I was a child here, Peter. In this room and playing out on that muddy street and walking up to the graveyard and the Anglican mission and inventing games on the boats and

50

canoes. And they used to put up a screen in the hotel and we sat on benches and watched old movies.'

In the darkness of the small room they lay still and spent and listened for the music. The house was behind Fraser's store and near the hotel, and in the cast-off wooden hotel, abandoned months ago when the new town was built, in the room that had been the dining-room the Eskimoes were holding a drum dance.

'He asked me to take you away,' Peter said. 'Your father. He said you have to go.'

'Is that a variety of love too, Peter?'

'It started out as love, I think. That's the funny part of it. The sad part.'

'And did you say you would? You'd take me away?'

'He didn't ask me if I would. He told me.'

'I'm not leaving. I have no place to go.'

'You have a big house. You told me he built you something that looks more like a castle than a house.'

'I couldn't fill it for him. He built it to be filled.'

'He told me to take you away. By force if I have to. Your father.'

The music was beginning. Someone in the crowded, square, unpainted room out beyond their dark and shuttered window was hitting a drum again — an Eskimo hitting with a curved stick a drum made of sealskin or the skin of a young caribou, dampened with water so it wouldn't break with a rise of frenzy, four Eskimoes each hitting a large flat drum, the bottom, one side then the other, tum-tum, tum-tum, a dancer rising, advancing onto the empty floor, shaking her head out of her parka hood, beginning to dance, sing, to mimic, acting out a story as she dances; a story of snow, of a swan, of a hunter: other dancers join her on the floor, learn her words, her gestures, hypnotized by the frenzied, controlled drumbeats: in the hot room a bystander shouts his shared joy and tension —

'Widow,' Kettle said. 'No husband. No children.'

They had joined the dance two hours ago, half by accident, half by design, after they fled Gordon Fraser's switch from joy to rage – his drunk stumbling rage to make his terrifying isolation an absolute that was no longer unbearable because it could become no worse. They walked in and four old men were pounding the big flat drums.

'Lover,' he said to the pearl in her ear-ring. The pearl that Hornyak had given her. 'But you have a lover.'

She laughed softly in the darkness and the sound of the drums. 'You know something. In all those six years. He didn't tell me where his home was. No relatives phoned to say they were passing through town. No mail came. Nothing.'

'I can think of worse fates.'

'But one time he said about you, "That lucky bastard, Pete. His ma had a family tree you could hang a thief on and not notice him." '

'He was making fun.'

'But he wasn't. He couldn't make fun about that.' She moved her head and kissed his chin.

'I am,' Peter said. 'I'm a lucky bastard.'

'And they're dancing,' she said. 'Because all the men are going to leave. They're going out to the mountains to hunt caribou and they leave their families here.'

'So they dance?'

'Dancing says it. I shouldn't have gone to the dance. Not so soon.'

'You were so beautiful when you danced.' He kissed her ear. 'And they all stopped and watched you and the old drummers laughed and pounded and everybody clapped until you ran into my arms.'

'They knew me when I was a child. I danced for them when I was a child. I loved the old dances. But now they hardly dance any more.'

'My God,' he said, 'you were beautiful. And that first song, that made them start by laughing – '

She hummed with the drums in the background, and then she sang softly: ' . . . kon-ous-suk-pun-ga – '

'Go on,' he said.

'Sou-pau-tee-ga Pee-ing-a-ya-ya-ya. It's silly.'

'What does it say?'

'It's a hunter's joke on himself. He went out hunting caribou and missed a shot and came home with nothing, and he
says he found out that his rifle was bent. He blames the gun,
but he knows what everyone's thinking.' She raised her hands
over the sheets and began to gesture in the near darkness. 'It's
the gestures, really, not the words. Mike hated the song.'

'You should have gone on forever,' he said.

'It was those deckhands. And the skipper and the mate. Coming in drunk, and trying to make the drummers play something so they could dance with the girls. All of a sudden I
had to leave.'

She touched his chest. 'You should have taken your shirt
off. It'll be all wrinkled.'

'I didn't have time,' he said.

'You're so skinny, Pete.' She touched his ribs and slid her
hand over his belly. 'You're so big and so skinny. You should
eat more.'

Someone stirred in the kitchen. A door creaked and a chair
scraped on the floor. 'Where are they?' a voice wanted to know,
hoarse and sleepy.

'They went out. Rosalie Elias came by for tea, and she said
they were at the dance.'

'I heard something in that bedroom.'

'They went to the dance, Gordon. It was your dog. At the
outside door. Lie down again. I'll make you some tea.'

'If they're behind that door and I catch them I'll kill the
two of them.'

'I'll make you some tea, Gordon.'

'Can't she do anything right? Can't she be a widow right
even?'

'I've been here all evening. Go back to bed.'

Fraser was silent. A door opened and a dog whimpered. 'Now,
now,' Fraser said. 'You mustn't make strange.'

The Eskimo woman was closing and locking the door.

'She's locking up,' Peter whispered. 'She doesn't know we're here.'

'Clara knows,' Kettle said. 'She heard us come in, I'm sure. She's been sitting out there, guarding us.'

'Earlier,' Peter said. 'There at supper when she followed him into the bedroom. He struck her, didn't he?'

'Yes,' Kettle said. 'When I was a girl, I used to wonder how she could stay with such a man. I knew they weren't married. When he got drunk he insulted her. But she wouldn't leave. I asked her why, and she said, some day I hope you know.'

Peter turned onto his back and lay motionless, his head touching in the darkness a lion that had not been knocked to the floor. 'I see,' he said.

'No,' she said. 'No, you don't. But now that it's past — I feel a life coming back. Something I had forgotten. He consumed me the way he consumed everything. You lived for him, Peter. Either you lived for him or you stopped living.'

'But I should tell you,' Peter said.

'Touch me,' she said. 'Touch me the way you did before.'

Peter lay tense, his feet somewhere in the darkness finding the bed too short. He stopped her hand. 'I should tell you. I said okay, I'll turn the damned handle and pump you some air. But just as he was crawling down into the barge I asked a question. I said Hornyak, I'll pump all day if you'll do this: can you lend me a hundred dollars? And he didn't laugh. Or ask me why. He just said, I'll come up and tell you when I think of an answer.'

And Kettle moved her hand now, would not be stopped. She insisted with the tips of her fingers and Peter continued: 'He was coming up to answer my question. Coming up to rest, the others say. But he never wanted to rest. He had no time to rest. He was coming up to answer. And that killed him.'

'It's gone away,' she said.

'I'm thinking,' he said.

'Don't think, Peter. Want me. Now.'

'I wanted him dead.'

54

From far outside came voices chanting, high, sad, mournful, chanting till sunrise and departure.

'Want me now,' Kettle said. 'You're going to leave, I know. I can tell.'

'He was climbing up to tell me. No, Kettle.'

'Touch is real,' she said. 'Touch is how we can know.' And she moved his hand, 'Touch me there.' She bent and kissed him. 'I taste you. I smell you. Even in all the darkness.' Her hands and her mouth found him.

And he touched her then, her breasts, his hand touching the damp of her thighs.

'Peter?' she said.

He turned roughly upon her.

'Peter?' she was saying. 'Peter?'

'I'm here.' And he moved. 'In a way, I killed him.'

She put a hand to his mouth. 'Touch me,' she said. And then she did not stop his mouth and softly she moaned, her arms clinging to his body, her arms tight, clinging to the surety of his flesh, to the sweat and pulse of his knocking body.

The frozen rain rattled on the hood of his parka, shutting out the sound of the sea. He walked along the cold gravel beach between the Arctic Ocean and the jumbled shacks of Tuktoyaktuk, trying to get far enough away from the boat so he could think. Trying to find somewhere on this flat, treeless coastline where, when he looked around, the mast of the *Nahanni Jane* would not be there pointing up at the stark grey sky.

He was afraid he could not endure the isolation for another day, for another hour even. He wondered why he had left Kettle at all. He could have stayed in her room and the boat would have sailed without him. But at dawn, as a deckhand alone on the deserted beach bent to release the headline, Peter went up the gangplank. He didn't need the money that a little more work would bring. He owed little allegiance to the captain. And he knew also that he did not leave because of Kettle's answer to his question about the future; she would stay with her father — until something happened, she said. Until something happened. He had departed impatiently from her submission to a dumb fate, knowing all the time that he did not know why he himself must get back to the boat.

The crew's delight in being away from Aklavik, and in having arrived at the coast, made Peter's isolation worse; for them, pumping off the barges and unloading the deck-freight, the journey to home would begin now in a matter of minutes. They were recklessly joyous at their work, forgetting that going home meant eleven hundred miles of river and a lake to cross before they could leave the boat and board a plane.

Tomorrow would be October the first. But if the weather held, and if their luck held, in two weeks they'd be in Yellowknife. Now he hated the idea of that good fortune. In two weeks the skipper would be off to Vancouver, to his wife and three kids and a TV set. The chief would pick up his Cadillac in Hay River and drive and drive until he was in Florida or California — or anywhere that wasn't Winnipeg and the woman who deserted him to live with another man. Pottle might or might not make it this time and fly to St. John's, to spend his money on the whores he had cursed all season. The cook would be back in Edmonton, drinking beer all day in the King Eddie. And he had agreed to take his regular job.

The thought was nearly unbearable, for it meant he would extend and fix this day's pain and make it into his future. Unless Kettle joined him. It was he who had burst back to life. And the birth was a throbbing awareness of his isolation. The sea and the landscape fading off into a grey mist of frozen rain made a giant cage in which he could not grasp the bars to shake them. He was alone. And if she chose to ignore his message, the boat would go on south past the Aklavik turn-off and he might never see her again. 'PLEASE,' he had radioed. 'PLEASE MEET —'

He shut out the thought from his mind and walked on, the mast still behind him. Grey driftwood, piled thick and tangled into a cove, made it impossible to follow the gravel beach and he turned inland, reluctant to meet the people who might be walking the single track that ran through the settlement.

He was to relieve a shore agent, in Yellowknife or Fort Smith or Hay River — relieve some man who was talking now of being bushed and who wanted to get out to civilization for a few weeks.

He had tried going out that first fall; but he got to Edmonton and couldn't leave the airport building. He was on his way east, he thought. But he couldn't change airports. He walked out to the circle in front of the terminal in Edmonton and looked at the string of bright yellow taxis waiting to whisk him away, and when a bent wiry man picked up his suitcase he snatched it back and fled into the building — out of the late October sunshine, out of the world of autumn and football games and roaring traffic — and he slept in a chair until he could catch the next plane going anywhere into the North.

Each fall he relieved a shore agent and had little to do but wait until late winter. Then the boats had to be prepared and the cat trains rumbled in with the first freight and the trucks bounced in over a winter road, beginning to stockpile supplies for the feverish season ahead. The ice, seven feet thick by spring, would not take heavy loads until late January, and he sat out the early winter in the little settlements behind a desk and close to an oil stove, thumbing through the mail and taking an order once in a while. He read everything he could find, listened to a short-wave radio, but he was no longer tempted to go outside to the world he reached through reading and listening. He did not even mix much with the people of the settlements. They thought him a little strange, the goldminers of Yellowknife, the government people of Fort Smith, the transportation people in Hay River — after a while they invited him because he was white and one of them and somehow not a drunkard or a sponge — yet they were surprised when he showed up at a party or at the curling rink or in the beer-parlour.

And when the boat's whistle blew he would begin the return trip to that winter life.

Log cabins, built of driftwood that came down the Mackenzie to be washed up in great rafts here twenty-five miles from the river's mouth, were sprinkled in an orderless fashion along the shore of the L of land that made the harbour. Their roofs were simply flattened tin cans or boards or sod, now covered with dry weeds. Sleigh dogs were staked out in groups, six or seven to a team. On a stoop stood a power washing-machine. A sleigh lay on its side in front of a door; another was thrown up on the roof of a cabin. An old woman, a pipe in her mouth, watched from a small square window, then saw that she herself was being watched and ducked behind a flour-sack curtain.

And the old house, he thought, was torn down to make room for a highway. His father only mentioned briefly in a note that he'd sold the house for a good price and had taken an apartment downtown. To be handy to everything, he said — his office and his bowling alley. Making fun of his surrender. His wife, a month before her death, had persuaded him to get rid of the Graham-Paige. Now he had no car. The home Peter had to go back to was a scattering of relatives who disapproved of riverboats and who would remind him that he came of what they called a good family. And they would shake their heads and watch him spend his money.

For he had money to spend. Men told each other and sometimes themselves that they came north for money, and by that criterion he was a success. In six years he had accumulated a few thousand dollars — he hadn't bothered to find out how many, for his cheques went to a bank. And now for the first time he felt the temptation to spend.

If Kettle didn't join him he would do something wild and extravagant, something that by its sheer extravagance would dull his mind and senses. Like a prospector who has struck it rich, he would blow it in. He'd take a room in the best hotel. That was one dream of the North; to take a room for a month in the Selkirk or the King Edward or the Macdonald, and to give parties for all your old pals and all the pretty waitresses and salesgirls, and to ring up for more booze and leave ten-dollar tips and keep a taxi waiting while you go to a double feature; and to try on a pair of shoes and tell the clerk to wrap up six pair, and to buy clean shirts by the dozen and throw the dirty ones away.

The Hudson's Bay post and the graveyard made a kind of centre to the settlement. And the graves too, with their crooked white wooden crosses or flat boards rounded on top to look like stones, and the individual picket fences to keep out dogs and wolves, were set at every angle to each other, like a crowd of ghosts met to gossip and visit here awhile, here beside the black stretch of arctic water, beneath a bleak grey sky that soon would be sunless for months.

But he was alone. The oil would soon be pumped off. The boat would shortly come to the H.B.C. dock to pick up a large wooden barge that was left by a bigger boat, the *Huskie,* earlier in the season. Some Eskimo men, under Pottle's direction, were already loading machinery into the white house, set like a big warehouse on the deck of the red wooden barge: caterpillars and packers and rollers and turnapulls that were used to repair the landing-strip outside the settlement. The strip was finished but still not in use, because of the weather.

Frozen rain rattled on Peter's parka hood. He passed two Eskimo women on the beach, taking dried whale meat off a high rack of poles. He waved and they turned away, and when he looked back again they were watching him.

He followed on past the two tiny missions, the Anglican and the Roman Catholic, and turned along the foot of the upsidedown L that became finally a gravel spit pointing out into the ocean toward a bare island that helped frame the harbour. Here there were more racks for drying fish and the meat of white whales, but they were empty now. Half a dozen teams of big white dogs were staked out in neat rows. There was the smell

of dung and rotten fish. Out here on the spit, in the summer-
time, the wind kept down the flies – the bulldogs and black-
flies and mosquitoes. The dogs uncurled and stood up, gaunt
and alert, straining at their leashes.

A tent was set up near the end of the spit. A white wall
tent. A tin chimney protruded through a hole in the roof.
The tent was set up on a frame of two-by-fours, and today
there was not enough wind to make it billow. On the beach,
on the ocean side, an old woman in a long dress was picking up
sticks of firewood. She now had all she could carry, and as she
was about to enter the tent she signalled to a man out in a
rowboat lifting a fish-net. The rowboat was inside the harbour.

Peter walked down to the beach as the Eskimo landed, and
without speaking began to help him catch the flapping fish,
crooked-backs and char and inconnu, and put them into two
buckets. They each picked up a bucket.

'Lots of fish today,' the Eskimo said. He was wearing a base-
ball cap under the hood of his parka, the peak set at a jaunty
angle.

'Big ones too.'

'You want some?'

'No. Thank you.'

'I give you some good crooked-back.' He set down his pail,
prepared to clean a fish on the spot.

'I don't want any.' Carrying the pail was making Peter
breathe hard. 'Just thought I'd give you a hand.'

'Makes the dogs fat.' The Eskimo hesitated, then picked up
his pail and grinned. 'Me too.'

'But you brought in your net.'

'We must leave today.' The Eskimo pointed to the first of
three small schooners. Aboard it were a dozen or so dogs and
two sleighs. But the usual oil-drums weren't lashed to the rails.

'Where're you off to?'

The Eskimo pointed north. 'Banks Island. Good white fox.
Stay two years. Much money.'

'Need a deckhand?'

The Eskimo grinned again. Then they ducked into the tent. The old woman was mixing flour and water in a tin bowl. A young woman, sixteen or seventeen, sitting on one of the two cots in the tent, her dress open, was nursing a baby. The child sucked ravenously at the small naked breast. The woman, watching the child, didn't look up. The man bent to kiss the baby and when he straightened and turned Peter saw for the first time the other side of his face, the scar tissue; he had at one time had his face torn by a dog.

'Time for tea,' the Eskimo said. 'You help me. Now you have some tea.'

'I'm waiting for the whistle. The boat's whistle.'

'We can hear it.' The Eskimo set out two mugs on the cooler side of the stove.

Peter couldn't quite stand up in the tent and he sat down on an empty apple-box. He could hear the dull drumming of the frozen rain on the tent. He caught the baby's eye and reached out to shake a small bare foot and the mother would not watch him but watched the baby.

'Listen,' the Eskimo said.

Peter raised his head. 'Wind?'

'Your boat. The whistle.' The Eskimo was holding a pail while the old woman dumped in tea-leaves.

'Sure you don't need a deckhand?' Peter said.

The Eskimo turned to Peter and grinned briefly. The scarred side of his face couldn't laugh. 'Can't go today.'

'Too late to strike out? But the water's perfect. In a day or two — '

'Can't go anyhow.'

'What's the matter?'

'Policeman.' He gestured off to where the R.C.M.P. barracks must be. 'Says I must pay the Hudson's Bay before I go. Poor trapping last year.'

'But you've got to go,' Peter said, 'to make any money.'

The Eskimo pointed around the tent. 'Must take my family. Policeman says leave them here.'

The boat's whistle sounded once more, abrupt and sad. Peter stood up, his head brushing the tent. It was time to go. But south this time. Time to turn back. Time to find out if Kettle would join him; he pressed his eyes shut for a moment. 'PLEASE MEET NAHANNI JANE AT AKLAVIK TURN-OFF BY MIDMORNING LOVE PETE.'

Tomorrow morning.

He could not even be sure that she had received his message. He could go again and ask the Hudson's Bay factor if he'd managed to send it. But he'd asked an hour ago, and the man had had no luck. Or what was worse, this time he might have an answer; a reply saying once more, no, I must stay with my father. And then the dumb fate that he so despised would be his; he would not only wait for something to happen; he knew what would happen. He would again be running —

'Have you a piece of paper?' he asked.

The Eskimo put down the tea-pail and looked under the two cots and into the apple-box. But he could find nothing. When he shook his head Peter searched through his own wallet and found a receipt for a paid bill. For a fishing-rod he used one afternoon at the foot of the Rapids of the Drowned.

'A pencil of some sort?'

The Eskimo shook his head.

Peter found a stub of pencil deep in a pocket of his parka. He broke the wood away from the lead with a fingernail while the Eskimo brandished a butcher knife.

'What's your name?'

'What?'

'Your name. What's your name?'

'Lawrence.'

'Lawrence who?'

Again he pointed toward the north. 'Lawrence Firth of Banks Island.'

Peter turned the receipt over and spread it out on the back of a frying-pan and wrote on the creased paper the place and date and the name of a bank: and then he added: Pay to the

order of Lawrence Firth of Banks Island the sum of two thous-
and ($2,000.00) dollars. He signed the paper and held it out
to the Eskimo. 'I've got to run. You see this?'

'We can't read.'

'Just take it,' Peter said.

'Time for tea,' the Eskimo said.

'Goddamnit, just take this. It's for you. It's money. You can
leave.'

The Eskimo went on pouring sugar into the two mugs, hastily, spilling it. 'No. Not money.'

'Take it, for God's sake. You've got to. I'll tell the Hudson's
Bay man.' And he knew the Eskimo must take it or he would
be like Hornyak — the Hornyak he met that summer day on
the prairies — Hornyak wheeling bird-free through the dry prairies, a car to drive through the cooling nights, women waiting; lonely women in dry prairie towns, dreaming of an adven-
ture with a stranger who blazes like a comet out of the short
luminous night; beer to drink in little hotels where men cool
off after the dust and heat of a day's hard work. Guy needs
some cash. He could live like that for a season, for a year, seeking, free and seeking . . . and nothing would be enough to kill
the isolation. Nothing. Nothing to kill the nothing. 'Please,'
he said to the Eskimo, 'take this and you can *leave*.'

The Eskimo offered the mug of tea: 'And you take this,
please.'

'I'll trade you,' Peter said.

And formally they traded, the piece of paper, the cup of
tea; the Eskimo grinned his half grin and Peter was outside
the tent and running, still carrying the mug, the tea scalding
hot, the boat's mast stark on the low horizon.

'I'll timber him up, be Jaysus. I'll kick
him so full of holes he wouldn't hold cordwood.' Pottle fan-
ned his long arms at an imaginary victim. 'I'll boot his lazy —'

'You'll do his work,' Peter said, 'the way you've just been doing. And then you'll come up here and bitch and moan and belly-ache.'

Young Jimmie Kartuk had ignored the boat's whistle and the mate was a man short on his deck crew. He had just now helped start the pump on the wooden barge, to pump out water that was leaking into the old hull, and he sat on the high stool with his wet knees pressed to the pilot-house radiator and he cursed. 'Like a rat off a sinking ship. Suffering Mary, you've got to pick men like you pick sleigh-dogs, by the size of the arsehole.'

'Amen,' a voice said, the voice disguised.

Pottle whirled around. The two deckhands playing cribbage on the counter greeted him with angelic smiles.

'Who said that?'

Neither Mud nor Abraham would answer.

'I said who said that? Or do I have to start my kicking right here?'

Still no answer.

'And they wonder why pigs eat their young.' Pottle turned to his steaming knees, muttering under his breath. 'The world is full of dirty bastards, and some of them bathe once a day.'

'Not me,' Mud said.

'You young punks are getting too damned sassy since we started south. You ought to take a lesson from Guy, here. He don't open his mouth to give a man the time of day.'

To the starboard on a clear afternoon they might have seen, far across the delta, the Richardson Mountains. But today Peter couldn't make out the turn-off into the Aklavik Channel. And the fog was getting heavier as the afternoon wore on, muffling and blinding them in a white shroud. He was standing beside the wheel, looking out intently through an open window. They were pushing the three barges in a row, *505* in the lead. The ocean had been so calm they pushed across to the Mackenzie's mouth without going on tow. But they hit fog opposite Reindeer Station and had been travelling at half speed ever since.

'I think he's in love,' Abraham said. 'He's been scratching himself in funny places.'

'He's thinking about his money,' Pottle said. 'Instead of piddling it away in a cribbage game he's saving it for his old age. He's going to die the richest man in the Northwest Territories and leave it all to me, so I can go on a six-month drunk in his honour.'

Mud hadn't had a haircut in two months and with a dirty hand he brushed the hair down over his eyes. 'Whose money were you spending last fall, mate?'

'It grieves me to say so, but a good half of it was my own. And I ran out after two months and eighteen glorious days, and I had to take a job cutting wood for a paper-mill till spring came along.'

'You worked last winter?' Abraham's fat cheeks threatened to bury his eyes. 'You said you went to Newfoundland.'

'Well, I almost did that too. Maybe I never clarified myself. But I'll be going this fall for certain.' Pottle again discovered that the two buttons were missing from his jacket. 'I woke up one morning with a trace of a dose, and the doctor told me not to travel.'

'Wish I'd got it instead of you.' Mud, sitting on the counter, kicked his heels violently against the wooden drawers at the thought of such good fortune.

Peter was watching the starboard shoreline; he took the boat farther out of the channel and closer to the shore.

'Mud my boy, you should have been born lucky instead of good-looking.' Pottle rubbed his steaming knees. 'I remember one time, I was sitting by this girl in a movie house in Edmonton there on Jasper Avenue. And pretty soon her elbow is bumping mine.'

'And all of a sudden she puts her hand on your knee,' Mud said.

'It's a God's fact, she did. She just lets her fingers drop ever so easy — '

'Into your pocket,' Abraham said.

'Just barely brushing my thigh. And I says to myself, what's this? She was a platinum blonde, a lovely girl, lonely in the big city — '

'And a strapping big fellow like yourself sitting next to her,' Mud said.

'I am, I am,' Pottle said. 'A gentleman, and the only legitimate son in a fine family of ten.'

'She took hold of your zipper,' Abraham said.

'It's a God's own fact. She just reaches over after I've been returning her nudges for a while, and as pretty as you please — '

'Hey!' Peter said.

'He recognizes the girl,' Mud said. And laughed wickedly at his own joke.

Johnny Louttit had come around from the side of the house on the house barge and was waving to get attention in the pilot-house and pointing forward into the fog.

Abraham straightened up from his hand of cards and looked. 'There's an iceberg up there and we're going to ram it head on and lose all hands before we can get the lifeboat down.'

'There's a dust storm heading this way,' Mud said. 'A good old Saskatchewan dust storm.'

'A plague of grasshoppers,' Pottle said. 'Whipped on by a herd of galloping polar bears.'

They all strained to see into the fog. Straining, they could here and there see eddies where there had seemed to be only stillness before. They were afloat in a pool of water that was somehow suspended in a world of fog. 'You make out anything?' Peter asked.

Abraham folded shut his hand of cards. 'Look.'

Peter turned his head quickly to where Abraham pointed straight ahead.

'It's a neon sign. The government just opened a big beer-parlour on a sandbar, and they want us to be the first customers.'

'And the beer will be free,' Pottle said, bending double to slap his wet knees, 'for any man who can eat two pounds of beefsteak smothered in mushrooms and fried onions.'

'And a pool hall on the side,' Mud said, 'with free snooker tables for deckhands under twenty-one. With big pockets . . .'

Then a freight canoe grew out of the white wall of fog, swinging parallel to the barges as it appeared, beginning to lose speed as it slowly closed with the boat.

'There's only trouble up ahead.' Pottle stood and moved away from the radiator to a window. 'Trouble enough for all of us.'

Peter reached back and a deckhand gave him the binoculars. A woman was seated in the bottom of the canoe, a blanket over her head. A man in Eskimo dress was sitting in the stern, handling the kicker. In the bow was a man with a fur cap on his head, a painter in his hands, crouched ready to grab the rail on the stern of the boat, the low rail that kept a tow-line from getting caught in the steering gear. Peter rang for slow ahead.

In a moment the skipper appeared in his shirt sleeves and bare-headed on the deck below the pilot-house and went to the forecastle entrance that sat like a little guard-house on the deck behind the capstan. He opened the two narrow doors and yelled down inside and waited for an answer. When it didn't come, he turned and climbed the ladder and came around to the side and into the pilot-house. He snatched the binoculars from Peter.

'You don't need the glasses to see who that is,' Pottle said. 'She keeps showing up like some kind of a haunting spirit that won't let us alone.'

'She don't mean no harm,' Mud said.

Pottle turned on him sharply. 'You young buggers are getting too big for your britches here lately.'

'She just needs a husband to bury,' the skipper said. 'So she can start on the next one.'

Peter looked out the back window to check the wash and make sure he had lots of water.

'Old Jonas,' Abraham volunteered. 'He's got this notion that the river is spooked. As long as – '

'Never mind old Jonas and his Indian stories.' The skipper banged the binoculars down on the counter and took the wheel from Peter.

Pottle went to the door. 'Any word from The Wells, skipper?'

'Not a syllable. Not hide nor hair of the man. You start to wonder if he really went overboard.'

'He did,' Peter said.

And now she was here and he had no plans to announce. The first rage of joy was hoarse in his throat and now he waited with nothing to say except that he could not endure to be without her. His lips were dry. She was here in answer to his message; in answer to his 'PLEASE MEET –' Here, now, and they would be together for two weeks, maybe three, going upstream, and then they would be in Yellowknife, and he would have his winter's decision to make. And once again there would be planes going south, and would he catch one this time and go all the way? For going to bed with a woman didn't mean he wanted to go to her house, her memories. Not if it meant playing puppet to a dead king. But no, that was over; God, they had erased that at least.

'I'll tell you something,' Pottle said. 'We're never going to make it now.' He went through the door and slammed it.

'Damned superstitious Newfie,' the skipper said. 'Ate so much codfish and boiled potatoes it addled his brain.'

'We better get down there,' Abraham said guardedly.

The two deckhands went out a door and Mud closed it quietly. The third deckhand, Louttit, came back from the house barge and the pump he was tending and onto the deck of the boat, and the three of them followed Pottle toward the stern.

Gordon Fraser stood up in the bow of the freight canoe and waved. When he was close enough he tossed the painter and

Pottle caught it and tied it to the rail. The canoe swung in and its gunwale hit the boat. Mud appeared awkwardly lugging an old tire that served as a fender, but he was too late.

'You better run down there,' the skipper said to Peter, 'and tell Fraser there's a storm forecast and he better hightail it for home or he'll end up skating.'

Peter went down the ladder and back toward the stern of the boat. He looked in at his own cabin, to see once more that he'd missed nothing in cleaning up. The sleeping-bag was rolled neatly at the head of the bare mattress. The green linoleum floor shone from his scrubbing. The wash-basin, though still not connected up by the engineers, after they removed a fitting one month ago, was glistening white. His clothes were crammed into the drawers under the bunk and only a few books and pencils and a clock and two dirty tumblers littered the small shelf over his sleeping-bag. About to close the door, he recognized a scrub-brush perched on his stool. He picked it up and dropped it overboard as he went back along the deck.

Fraser was handing up a suitcase to one of the deckhands. Kettle, taking off her blanket, bent down to hand it back from the stern of the *Nahanni Jane* into the canoe. She tried to speak to her father, but the crew crowded forward, asking him aboard.

'At least for some coffee,' the mate was saying. 'You must be froze stiff.'

'We can stop to make tea.' Fraser pointed to an empty syrup pail in the bottom of the canoe.

'It's on the stove. It's ready.'

'Dad,' Kettle said.

'We'll have to feel our way back to Aklavik. The fog is like wool in that channel.' Fraser pointed with a mitt back over his shoulder. 'Nuksana missed a turn back there, and we just about made a channel of our own.'

'Look,' Nuksana, the Eskimo, said. He picked a scrub-brush out of the water and handed it onto the boat.

'What the bloody hell?' Pottle said. He thought Kettle was

bending to retrieve the scrub-brush and pushed it into her hand.

Fraser pulled at the painter and released the knot. Nuksana, in the stern of the canoe, let go of the rail and the canoe drifted away and fell behind. Bending quickly the Eskimo braced himself and pulled the starter rope; but the kicker didn't start.

'Hey, dad,' Kettle called. 'Before you go.'

'You be good to yourself,' Fraser answered. His face creased for a moment with pain. He took off his cap and doffed it and quickly pushed it back onto his shaggy grey hair. 'You send me a card when you get home.'

And then he saw Peter standing back of the crew. 'Mr. Guy,' he called. 'Mr. Guy, I want to thank you.'

'There's a storm coming,' Peter shouted. He pointed up at the fog-hidden sky. 'There's a bad one on the way.'

'I want to thank you,' Fraser called. The kicker on the stern of the canoe came alive. 'I want to thank you, Mr. Guy. There at supper — I judged you wrong. I want to apologize.'

'Get home fast,' Peter shouted.

'I say, Mr. Guy, you take care of that girl of mine. See that she gets on that plane at The Wells and out to the city.'

'Dad,' Kettle called.

The Eskimo swung the canoe toward the boat and Fraser turned and motioned him away. 'Have a couple for me,' he shouted. 'When you get to the bright lights.'

Peter cupped his hands to his mouth. 'There's a storm — '

'When you get outside to the bright lights,' Fraser shouted. He made a gesture suggesting that Peter have a drink.

Kettle touched Peter's shoulder. 'He can't hear you. He can't hear out there.'

Peter waved and Fraser waved back and both Peter and Kettle waved and the canoe was already a dim outline in the fog.

Kettle started to pick up her suitcase but Mud was waiting and took it. The crew turned away from watching the canoe. 'We were afraid', Kettle said, 'that you'd sneaked by us.'

'Mr. Guy there,' Pottle said, 'he's been looking holes in this fog for two hours. You'd almost think he knew you'd be wanting a ride out.'

Kettle smiled. 'I'm glad — '

But Peter was looking up at the pilot-house.

The skipper was leaning out a door. 'Get your ass back up here, Guy. I didn't tell you to take a vacation.'

Peter shrugged by way of apology to Kettle. 'The poor bastard must get lost in his own bathtub. So he's a riverboat skipper.'

Kettle had turned away, following Mud toward the cook's cabin.

They made good time for four days, running hard all day beneath a dying sun, running all night by moonlight and searchlight and the pilots' memories. Sometimes they hit patches of fog. But they only cut down to slow ahead and kept inching forward, inching south; and steadily they pushed on through a nearly deserted world. One time they swung off course to avoid a fat brown bear that was swimming across the river. Working upstream close in to the bank above Point Separation they saw a solitary moose one afternoon, and a little while later, three wolves.

They passed Arctic Red River, where the crimson fireweeds had gone to seed on the hill-side and the canoes were absent from the long muddy beach below the church on the hill. The shelters set up earlier in the summer to smoke fish were naked frames of poles now, the tents and the canoes and the busy women and running children and the squatting men all gone.

They worked slowly through the Lower Ramparts, up the long bend between three-hundred-foot banks of shale that sloped barren and steep to the river. And from there they faced two hundred miles of tricky channels, past shifting islands and sandbanks that left the positions marked on the charts, past the crumbled traders' shacks that had been Little Chicago, past Burnt Point and the Ontaratue River.

Two deckhands climbed the mast above the pilot-house to wave at the girls in Fort Good Hope; but only a limping Indian and an old bearded priest came to the edge of the hill to return the greeting. The deckhands entered the pilot-house dejected and Louttit answered gruffly to some teasing: 'Everybody's got enough sense to head into the bush.'

'Everybody's gone from the world,' Pottle added, and was forgiven for his teasing.

'Just all the women are gone,' Mud said.

'We still got to get Mud fixed up,' Pottle said. 'Wait till we circle down and see the lights of Edmonton spread out below us.'

'Why not Yellowknife?' Mud said. 'I got to stay with my sister in Edmonton.'

The Ramparts loomed before them in the nearing darkness, a yellow-brown wall of limestone; past the Ramparts and the hump of water they would have a fighting chance. They pushed on into the nightfall, labouring up the canyon, the river less than half a mile wide, the current strong and steady. They tied up under a rock overhang on the east shore; long ago a rockfall had made a little bank where a deckhand could go ashore and hook a headline onto a deadman the N.T. had placed there. Grass and moss and even some stunted spruce had established themselves on a few square yards of rock. It was pitch dark as the deckhand came back onto the barge; the searchlight beam touched the overhanging zig-zag of rock; the waterfalls were not running; the trees on the cliff above them were out of sight.

In the morning they left two barges and pushed the lightest one up and out of the canyon. The river had fallen more than they expected; it must be freezing far to the south. The big rock was four feet out of the water. On either side the water was dotted with smaller rocks and white with riffles indicating more hazards. The track for navigation was a narrow channel, and the water pouring through slanted down toward them and now dropped a good six feet.

They pushed *Barge 309* toward the hump alone; they pushed at the hump for one hour, two hours, as if at a stone wall, at the Ramparts itself; and when the stationary and mightily labouring *Nahanni Jane* seemed suddenly to break through and move forward, a foot, a yard, hesitating, then inching forward smoothly, then beginning to slide as if into a great breach, the crew whistled and cheered, the deckhands slapped each other and did a jig on the open deck.

But the elation was short-lived. Instead of driving on southward they advanced only a few thousand yards and tied the barge to a big tree on shore. A large shelf of ice extended from the east bank above the fast water, and they had to go up above it, to where the water ran fast enough to resist freezing, coming around a point. They put out a headline and made the barge secure; and then they unhooked and turned around and headed back to their two remaining barges. They hooked onto the big wooden barge, *505*, but by the time they were ready to approach the hump for a second time the cold sunshine of the afternoon was dying in the canyon. Already it was night, and the little sky they could see loomed ominous and black.

The snowstorm was slow in arriving. But it caught them on their second night in the Ramparts canyon. By morning the powdered snow had drifted in at the ill-fitting doors and windows and a silt of snow lay on Peter's window-sill, on the foot of his bunk and on his shorts and trousers; the cabin was icy cold in spite of the knocking radiator. He swore when he put his feet on the bare linoleum and Kettle zipped the sleeping-bag shut behind him, refusing to get up for breakfast. She refused to answer when he asked her, from the open door, if she wanted coffee.

Peter went down to the galley and returned twenty minutes later, carrying a basin of hot water from the boat's washroom. He set it on the white porcelain sink in a corner of his cabin and prepared to shave, not taking off his parka. He lathered the brush furiously in his shaving-mug and bent to the round mirror over the sink; and now in the concave surface he saw the blur of his head, his hair honied by summer sun, two swimming eyes, and the sharp distended outline of his nose. Hastily he flipped the mirror; Kettle's image dropped down from above and crowded against his shrunken face.

She wiggled up out of the sleeping-bag, out of the cocoon warmth of flannel and down. 'I'm sorry,' she said. 'I'm sorry I said it, Peter.'

'Forget it,' he said. 'Maybe it's a great idea.'

'But you won't come back to bed,' she said.

'I'm supposed to be out on deck. I'm supposed to be out there standing in the wind, getting snowed on.'

'That's why you're taking time to shave,' she said.

He stopped lathering his face and wiped the steam from the mirror; and he frowned at the smile that surprised him. 'So I had to come back. Remind me. Rub it in. The way I had to come hurrying back from Tuk.'

'Don't apologize,' she said.

'Why apologize?' he said. 'I'm the type, for Christ sake. I'm the goddamn saviour type. Back there in Tuk when I went running to catch the boat to come and meet you, I was so goddamned full of saviourism I had tears running down both cheeks.'

'I should have stayed in Aklavik,' she said.

'The hell you should have stayed in Aklavik. You couldn't have stayed in Aklavik. You had to come back once more, to look for the bastard.'

'Be kind, Peter. Be Peter the Great.'

'At the rate I'm going, I'll be Peter the Pater.'

'Not at the rate you're going this morning.'

'I've got to go stand in the snow,' he said.

'Be Peter the Peter,' she said. 'Come back to bed.'

He watched her in the mirror, her back to his faltering anger as she sat hunched, her arms crossed as if to clutch some invisible warmth to her breasts. 'Goose bumps become you,' he said.

'I'll wear them often when we get outside.'

'I'll get you some new ones,' he said.

'And I'll give my old ones to the cook.'

'Wonderful. She can wear them when she drinks in the King Eddie.'

'Hand me your big sweater, Peter.'

But he didn't move from the mirror. 'Give me two minutes. Two minutes to shave, and then I'll have two minutes left for private enterprise.' He touched the safety razor to the right side of his face. 'That hag of a cook is a regular bulwark of virtue since you came aboard. She'll soon have the skipper himself saying grace before meals.'

'She misses your business,' Kettle said. 'Tell her you'll soon be rid of me. Tell her that once we get to Norman Wells —'

'By the way,' he interrupted. 'I asked the skipper. As you requested. He'll radio that you'll pay for any further dragging operations.'

'I didn't ask you to ask, Peter.'

'Not at all,' Peter said. 'We talk about nothing but the future.'

'Have you been thinking about it, Peter?'

'When we're not doing it,' he said, 'I'm thinking about it.'

'Stop thinking then,' she said.

He picked a towel off the radiator and began to wipe his face. 'Pardon my boots, madam,' he said.

Kettle turned now to watch him. 'You missed the left side,' she said. 'And cut yourself.'

He went on rubbing the lather from his face, the right side clean and glowing, the left side stubbled. He did not move away from the mirror, but only tipped his head slightly, to look at the point of his chin, and he saw the small square window behind him, the frost that arching covered half the pane, the drift of snow beyond.

'In Yellowknife,' she said, 'you can have a private barber.'

'With your money,' he said.

Kettle didn't answer.

'We're freezing in right here,' he said. 'Sowbelly and pow-dered eggs for breakfast all winter; you'll never have to get up.' He saw now what Kettle had seen at a glance; he had nicked his chin, the scar on the tip of his chin. Carefully he avoided touching the bright bead of blood.

'Come to bed,' she insisted.

He did not turn toward her but watched in the mirror as she unzipped the bag; he saw the motion of her return into the bag's warmth, the mirrored darkness, the soft full brush of hair: 'You should borrow my razor,' he said. 'I'm getting a whisker burn.'

'Come to bed,' she insisted.

'In Yellowknife,' he said, 'I can have a private doctor for my private whisker burn.'

'I'm sorry for what I said,' she said.

'What the hell,' he said. 'I could run the whole show.'

'The whole show.' She was snuggling down into the bag. 'Certainly, Peter.'

'I know this boat. I know the fishermen. I know the river, the lake. I know the very fish themselves.'

'I've tried to apologize,' she said, only her mouth and eyes showing.

'I know the very people who ate the very fish that made the very Mr. Hornyak very rich.'

'Very rich,' Kettle said.

'I know he knew what he wanted. Hornyak knew, by God. Exactly. He even knew what I wanted.'

'What I wanted,' she said.

'Laugh,' he said. 'You should laugh. Maybe his clothes will fit me too. I always thought he was on the small side, but maybe everything will fit.'

'Everything will fit,' Kettle mocked.

And then she disappeared inside the sleeping-bag; he turned quickly from the mirror, to where he expected to find her face. She did not answer when he called, 'Kettle?' She did not stir, while he stood watching; and then he could not turn back to his basin of water. He went stepping softly in his big boots toward the door.

The problem was simple. For a distance of five hundred yards the water came over the hump at the rate of eight knots. The *Nahanni Jane*, pushing a loaded barge in dead water, could make a speed of eight knots. Pushing an empty barge she could theoretically gain on the current. But the wooden barge, bigger and heavier than the others to begin with, was partially loaded.

'We haven't got a chance,' Arnafson said. 'We can't possibly get through the fast water pushing *505*, and here we sit freezing our balls off in this weather and pretending we're going to sail this stinking tub to that stinking town of Yellowknife.' He backed away from the galley table and dropped his cup in the sink without rinsing it; he turned and slouched into the engine-room, the old cap pulled low over his red eyes, and he closed the watertight door.

'Pour me some coffee,' McAlpine said to the deckhand nearest the stove. The deckhands were clustered around the galley stove, having coffee and trying to get warm. 'Let's have one more cup.' He pointed to the tin of canned milk. 'And let's have the tin tit, Guy.'

Now the mate came into the galley and bent over and brushed the snow out of his red hair.

'Have some coffee,' the skipper said. 'Then we'll give it a try.

Pottle went gloomily to the cupboard and took down a heavy white mug off a hook. He poured scalding coffee into the mug and added three spoonfuls of sugar. 'We should hook onto *301*, maybe. That wind out there is some bloody tricky.'

'Maybe it'll be calm tomorrow,' Mud said. He took a hand out of a glove to brush his hair under his cap. 'And cleared off maybe.'

'And maybe it won't.' Abraham was pretending to great meteorological insights this morning. By a pregnant silence he forecast the worst. He poured grapefruit juice into his empty coffee cup and drank it off at one swallow. The sourness made him grimace and the fat closed over his eyes.

'We'll take the wooden barge over,' McAlpine said, 'and get that out of the way. So bundle up and get ready.' He nodded toward Peter. 'Guy, if you help the deckhands, Jonas and I can handle the wheel.'

Pottle took a seat when a deckhand stood up. 'I'll be out when I finish this black excuse for coffee.'

Men who spent season after season on the river discovered once again that winter had come and they were unprepared. There weren't enough gloves and heavy jackets and caps and boots to go around. So they swore at the weather and the captain and put on three shirts instead of two and two pairs of trousers instead of one, and out they went into the wind.

The fine snow had drifted into the folded tarpaulins and into the coils of line. The wind swept the decks clean, but the bare metal was cold to the touch, and the driven snow whirled down into the canyon and cut at their eyes.

They threw off the lines that tied the wooden barge to *301*, a line freezing moments after it got wet, and in turn the lines soaked their gloves and they too froze stiff. McAlpine had trouble getting the wooden barge away from shore; the wind caught the high barge like a sail and set it in. It was eleven o'clock by the time they pushed up to where the fast water began.

When they came up even with the foot of the rock, out of

the nearly dead water of the whirlpool at the bottom of the rapids, the skipper rang the engine-room asking for the superchargers. The two Vivians, four-hundred-horse and eight-cylinder marine engines left over from World War Two, were equipped with superchargers that would give them a little extra power for a short period of time. Peter, in the big, cold, dark house on the barge, keeping out of the wind with the deckhands, felt the tremor go through the old barge as the superchargers came on.

'I'll bet we get through in no time,' Mud said. He stared out of the half-opened barge door at the rock and the skyful of snow. 'I'd sure like to get some mail. When we get to The Wells, maybe there'll be mail waiting.'

'Harvest will be over,' Abraham said, 'before you get any mail this year. Get used to that now.'

'We should be watching for signals,' Mud said. He was ashamed of his moment of homesickness.

'Let him blow that whistle. He loves to hear the damned thing.' Abraham was looking for a place to sit.

'We might as well paddle,' Louttit said despairingly. 'Or hold up our coats for sails.' He had wrapped a scarf around his head and a button nose marked the centre of the circle that was his face.

'If I had a coat to hold up.' Abraham was wearing two bright plaid shirts over a dress shirt, all of them stuffed into his trousers. He had put on moccasins and rubbers in place of his usual boots, and his old beret was pulled down to cover the tips of his ears. 'Where's *your* winter wardrobe, Mud?'

Mud was wearing torn jeans and a jacket from which he had removed the sheepskin lining on a hot day. He had outgrown both in the course of the season. 'I sent my money home for the folks to keep.'

'I thought you were your own boss. A stud like you.'

Peter climbed up and sat on the seat of a caterpillar. He could see through the door to the rock and the storm. He picked out a crevice in the rock and watched it. The crevice was above the water and dry and the snow drifted inside made it a dazzling white.

'I still bet we make it,' Mud said. 'I'll buy everybody a drink in Yellowknife when we get there, if they don't throw me out of the beer-parlour.'

'I was talking to Jonas last night,' Abraham said. 'He seen a barge break in half here one fall. It came over the rapids and hit that still water of the whirlpool — that water going the wrong way — and it busted in half like a twig.'

Mud said he didn't believe a word of it.

'The hell you don't believe it. He said in the old days when they floated them sturgeon-head scows down — he said it was nothing for a scow to go to pieces in the fall. You just hung on to the steering sweep and dog-paddled till another outfit fished you out. If you didn't freeze to death and drown.'

Mud looked to Johnny Louttit for the voice of sanity.

'I heard a lot of stories,' Louttit said. He was still embarrassed or astonished by his own previous moment of despair. 'My cousin was on the old *Distributor* before the war. He said they burned four loads of wood one fall, and every time they just about got to the top of the hump the stern paddle came up too high and back down they went again. And by that time they'd have to go ashore and chop more wood, 'cause all the wood-piles were burnt up by then. That was before the war.'

'But they made it,' Mud said.

'I don't remember what he said.'

'And she was a big sternwheeler,' Abraham put in. 'The smaller ones here used to rip off paddles and tear down smoke-stacks and get stove in and everything else.'

The discussion of their inevitable defeat went on until the cook showed up to denounce the weather and to say she wasn't going to keep dinner warm all the rotten afternoon while they gabbled like a flock of geese. After dinner Mud was mad or hurt and went up to the bow to watch their progress and Louttit fell asleep in the cab of a turnapull and Abraham stayed in the galley, the skipper be damned, to drink coffee and to keep warm.

Peter watched the crevice in the worn rock. He looked out from the calm dark interior of the deck-house at the rock and the grey chaos above it. They were making progress. Enough progress to keep them trying and not enough to get them to their destination. He wanted to sneak away from his responsibility and go back to the boat and be with Kettle in his cabin. Desire stirred his chilled body. If they got past the Ramparts, they would quickly get to Yellowknife. Even if Kettle flew out from Norman Wells, the boat would be in Yellowknife soon after. In ten days at the most. But something remained unresolved. He wondered and watched the rock.

He watched until the afternoon began to fade, and when he started back toward the pilot-house he guessed they had moved forward something under fifteen yards.

And then as darkness closed in they began to drop back to spend their third night in the canyon. Just enough light lingered on the water above the hump so that a deckhand coming up to the pilot-house for orders spotted the canoe long before it got to the boat. Jonas picked up the binoculars and studied the river for a while. At first he said there were only giant snowflakes to be seen. Then he reported to the skipper and to Peter that there were two men in the canoe. He watched again for a while and reported that they were paddling too fast for men who had a long way to go; but maybe they were trying to get to Fort Good Hope before complete darkness overtook them in the canyon.

The *Nahanni Jane* drifted downstream. As she passed the spot where *Barge 301* was tied up, small beneath the overhanging cliff, McAlpine rang for full ahead and they began to move forward to land and tie up.

'Tomorrow,' McAlpine said. 'Tomorrow we start at the crack of dawn, storm or no storm. None of this coffee-drinking stuff. Another hour and we'd have made it.'

'But not with this wind,' Jonas said. He put down the binoculars. 'Nick a wheel on a rock so we have to run one engine slow, and we won't get the boat through, let alone a barge.'

'One bloody more hour and I'd have been over,' the skipper insisted. He began taking the boat to port side now, watching to see how the barge moved in the shifting drafts. 'Ten yards more. Five yards even. Like yesterday. All of a sudden you're moving.'

Twenty yards, Peter thought. He shook his head at Jonas and tried to approach the subject tactfully. 'The old *Pelican Rapids*. She used to run up alone through the rapids and lay a cable and four men on the hand capstan made the difference.'

'And the *Richard E.*,' Jonas said. 'And some of the Radium boats. They tried everything, but they ended up winching.'

'And they lose half a day laying a cable,' the skipper said. He dismissed the subject. 'How much water in that barge, Guy?'

'Pottle says he'll have to pump till midnight.'

'Old oakum,' the skipper said. He rang the engines to slow ahead as the wooden barge eased up beside *301*. The reefer on *301* disappeared behind the slowly advancing deck-house.

'Old oakum,' Jonas said. 'And rotten wood.'

The three deckhands had just finished tying up when the canoe came into the canyon. Louttit, always conscientious, was going up to check the headline on *301*, but now he turned back. There were two canoes. The first was towing a second and smaller canoe. The skipper rang the engines off and the boat fell silent except for the wind and an occasional rattle of pans. The cook was irritated at having people in her galley all day. There was the clanging of a steel door and the chief appeared shortly on deck in his shirt-sleeves and met the captain on the forward deck.

'The only thing warm on this boat is the bearings on those two shafts. And if you keep those two superchargers running wild all day tomorrow so that we can stand still out there in the river we might as well sell this stinking tub for scrap iron.'

'Keep them cool,' the skipper said. 'That's your job. That's what you're getting paid more than union rates for. Piss on them, chief.'

But the chief didn't answer. Both men stopped talking and turned, the snow stinging their faces, and they watched the canoe. Instead of going on by it began to swing toward the boat. The man in the stern used his paddle as a rudder for a moment; then they were both paddling again, working too hard for men who knew better.

'Rabbit-skins,' Jonas said. He started toward the stern of the boat.

The two Indians looked inadequately dressed in their old tweed caps and red neckerchiefs and dark windbreakers. By the time they were abreast of the wooden barge they were pointed upstream; the smaller ratting canoe came to the end of its tow-line and it too turned.

As the forward canoe fell back to the stern of the boat the crew members gathered to watch. The chief, shivering in his shirt-sleeves, tugged his engineer's cap low over his eyes. Peter had on no cap.

'You're going to freeze that high forehead of yours, Guy,' the chief said.

'Means he's smart,' Abraham said. 'Smart enough to keep warm at night.'

'Grass doesn't grow on a busy street,' Pottle said.

The Indian in the bow of the canoe wouldn't let Pottle take the painter. He himself held on to the rail of the boat. He turned and said something in an Indian tongue to his companion. The Indian in the stern of the canoe stood up, half crouching, and gave Peter the end of the long line that ran to the second canoe. Then he said: 'We are going to our traplines. We were hunting for meat.' He gestured down toward the second canoe. 'But we find — on a sandbar caught in some driftwood. We must go now.'

The Indian in the bow saw his companion nod and he let go of the boat's rail. The canoe began to drift away. Jonas

84

yelled to the two men in Slavey and then in French.

'Et vous avez trouvé la mort?'

The man in the bow answered briefly.

'Hey, your canoe,' Pottle shouted.

The man in the stern of the canoe shook his head. 'No good now,' he called.

Peter was pulling in on the tow-line that had been placed in his hands. He pulled and the small canoe came up slowly beside the stern of the *Nahanni Jane* and the men crowded to the rail.

'They saw we can't make it,' Arnafson said. 'They want us to try this.'

'What did he say?' McAlpine said to Jonas.

'He said there were tracks. A bear must have got at the face – '

And then the stench of the body hit them. They reeled away, staggering back across the deck to the port side. Only Peter did not run, for he was holding the line. The wind had thrown an old quilt back and snow lay in the folds of the quilt and a hand and an arm lay exposed. An electric light cord was wrapped around the arm and the hand. The lamp was gone from the cord. The arm was bare and the flesh was a grey-white. And on the flesh of the forearm was a tattoo of a ship in full sail.

'Jesus H. bleeding Christ,' the skipper said.

Then Kettle screamed. She had come up behind the men from Peter's cabin and had joined them on the stern. She was standing forward from Peter, near the rail and beside the life-boat. She could see into the canoe. She screamed and then she ran at Peter and began to pound at his back, his arms, with her clenched white fists. He couldn't let go of the line, for the current tugged hard at the canoe. 'You did it!' she scream-ed. 'You did it! You did it! You gave him that light and you killed him!'

She dodged past Peter and started toward the canoe. She was at the low rail and bending forward when young Mud

85

stepped close behind her and caught her in a great awkward hug. And then she fell silent.

'Take her to her cabin,' the skipper said. 'The cook's cabin. And let's get this thing aboard.'

Their first passion was to get to

Norman Wells. In the morning, at dawn and in the driving snow, they gathered on the wind-swept decks, jovial, eager to desperation. An intense thrill of release was on them; they had recovered the body. Now they had only to deliver it to Norman Wells. Men who had listened in the long night were obscene and easy now, in their laughter at the freight on the stern deck.

And in the driving snow they took the *Nahanni Jane* over the hump of water without a barge; they found the old deadman on the point a mile above the hump — a loop of wire running from a timber buried in the permafrost. They laid seven thousand feet of wire down to and over the hump, through the narrow and turning channel, and they buoyed the end with a steel drum. At noon they went into the canyon and once more picked up the wooden barge. They pushed the barge up to the bottom of the hump and picked up the drum and wire with pike-poles and a lariat of line, and they took five turns around the head of the hand capstan on the bow of the barge. And with Jonas at the wheel and the second in the engine-room, they pitted their strength against the oppressive current.

They put four wooden bars into the capstan-head and four men at a time bent to the task, their bodies parallel with the wooden deck as they pushed, one man holding the wire tight on the capstan-head, hoping to reel it in.

They moved forward easily at first, making a few yards in half an hour. Then Arnafson, helping on deck because the second engineer had a club-foot and could not help, slipped and fell. 'Goddamn this goddamn ice.'

The snow was packing hard and slippery under their feet. Louttit went away silently to find a pick or an axe.

'I'll spell you, chief,' Pottle said. 'Take this wire and just hang on.'

'I'm an engineer.' Arnafson sat down on a bitt. 'We've got this whole goddamn thing backwards – all of us sweating up here on the barge and the corpse sitting back there on the boat.'

Captain McAlpine, built, as he was fond of explaining, like a brick shit-house, straightened up from where he was rolling line onto a wooden drum. The muscles in his jaw were working like the nose of a rabbit. 'Go on then. We can do it without you.' He motioned the chief back toward the boat. 'Go on back to your engine-room. You can loaf all afternoon. We'll call you for supper.'

Arnafson tugged at the beak of the engineer's cap that he didn't take off even at meal-time or in his bunk, as if the top of his head was to be forever a mystery. 'You can't run away from a corpse doing this.'

'Who the hell's running away?'

'You're running away. You and everybody else. You want to run away but you won't let go of that bloody damned ghost stretched out back there on the stern of the boat.'

The skipper looked around at the raised heads, his small eyes restless in his big face. He confronted the inquiring men and they glanced away. 'Go on back to your engine-room, chief.'

'That's where I'm going,' the chief said. He pulled off his gloves and stood motionless.

'Well go, then. Get your ass moving in that direction before I move it for you.'

The chief broke out cursing. He turned away, and before he disappeared around a corner of the deck-house he stopped and hurled back once more: 'You can't run away from a corpse doing this. You can't even get south doing this.'

'Good riddance to bad rubbish. Come on you lucky devils.' McAlpine took hold of a capstan-bar. He was an impatient man; his will brooked little contradiction or delay. But when the opposition yielded he lost confidence. His bullying turned, on its victory, to vacillation. Having made his point he couldn't see how anyone else could find it valid. 'Come on!' he shouted now, trying to sound confident. 'Let's go, boys!'

They gave a heave together and the capstan-head turned inside the coils of line. The dogs clicked sharply on the base of the capstan.

'Easy, me lads,' Pottle said. 'You're wasting your mother's milk. Keep it slow and easy.'

Louttit came back with a pick. Small and industrious and quiet, he began to chip away at the ice, giving them secure toe-holds. The skipper fell silent and applied his bull strength to the capstan-bar.

The water poured over the hump so endlessly that after a while each man, as he came around full circle and could look up and over the bow of the barge, stared in fascination at the rushing sheet of smooth water that was the channel. One man and then another looked to left and right, to the broad river above the entrance to the Ramparts. It quickly widened to a mile and a half and then to two miles, and they knew it stayed that way for thirty more; but the only navigable channel ran for two hundred feet along the side of a flat rock. They could hardly believe this was the only channel, the only way through. And yet they could see the big, flat, water-worn rock and more rocks beyond on their starboard, the ripple and flash of white water over unseen rocks on the port side. And they spelled each other, worked head down until their calves and shoulders ached and their heads throbbed, and they looked up and the sheet of smooth water came at them, carrying now pans of ice.

At three o'clock the cook brought out coffee and sandwiches. She looked for a while at the rush of water, at the decks white with packed snow, at the men who fell silently and greedily upon the coffee and food, their bodies rank with freezing sweat; she felt the dull insistent thudding of ice against the barge and she said 'Huh' and went back without her coffeepot to the galley.

'Easy bloody life,' Pottle said, 'being a woman.' But he got no response. 'Drink coffee in the galley or lock yourself up in a cabin like that Hornyak woman.'

'How is she?' McAlpine said abruptly to Peter.

'She won't let me in. She wouldn't this morning.'

The ice-floes came thicker in the late afternoon. The current, faster in the chute, tended to bring the floes down on the barge. The ice was new and hard, breaking loose from the shore somewhere above as the water dropped, and the hard, broken edges of the floes bumped the barge and cut into its wooden hull like the teeth of a saw.

Louttit went to check the pump over a well on the barge and came back shaking his head.

'Worse?' the skipper said.

'Leaking faster than ever.'

'In another hour we'll be over.'

'In another hour it'll be pitch dark,' Pottle said. 'And this crew is dead on its feet. From giving each other rides on this damned merry-go-round.'

'What would you do, Pottle? Quit like we did yesterday?'

'I'd look around', Pottle said, 'and see if there's any extra baggage we might be throwing overboard.' He bent and tried to take the capstan-bar from Peter but Peter went on working.

A hush fell over the bow. They kept inching forward in the falling gloom of the night and the storm, but they were waiting. Their figures were white with snow in the nearing darkness. The water out in front of them was black, except where a floe showed white with the snow it carried. Here in the shelter of the deck-house away from the wind the men could hear each other clearly, along with the sound of water and ice, but they could not hear the boat's engines and it seemed they were moving the barge by themselves. Or trying to. After a long pause McAlpine spoke again:

'We're keeping the body aboard.'

'We could take it back to Fort Good Hope,' Pottle said. 'There's a graveyard there. And a priest even.'

'We're not going back north. And we're not — we spent three days looking for it. Why?'

Abraham straightened up and rubbed at his ears. 'I'm not busting my ass out here for exercise. Let's deliver the goods.'

They were gaining a few inches again. Mud and Louttit took hold of a capstan-bar together, one man pushing, one pulling. The bar broke with a dull crack.

'Goddamnit, go easy,' the skipper said. 'We've only got two spares. And there's another barge to bring through.'

The big searchlight on top of the pilot-house flicked on and off at that moment, on and off again.

'Trouble on the boat? The engines maybe.' Pottle was sitting on the deck while holding the line tight on the capstan, and he moved again as if he must find somewhere a warm spot.

Louttit was picking himself up off the deck. The light flicked on and off, then it came on and stayed on, the bright beam over their heads filled with snow.

'Somebody better run see,' the skipper said.

91

No one moved away.

Louttit tightened the scarf he wore wrapped around his head. Searching in the near-darkness to find another capstan-bar, suddenly he shouted, 'Look! The ice!'

The searchlight, moving ahead of them, played on the snow-covered ice that had formed out from the shore in the slack water above the hump.

'It's broke loose,' Louttit shouted. 'It'll come down the channel.'

'We should let go,' Peter said.

'We're within twenty minutes of making it. Just hang on, boys. Don't panic over a little chunk of ice.'

'We should really let go,' Peter said.

'Look, you've got us in enough trouble, Guy. Let's all give her hell. We want to get to Norman Wells, don't we?'

They bent to the capstan-bars and the barge began to inch forward more rapidly. Now the great moving pan of ice came into the channel; it turned as the current caught its edge and it began to gain momentum. The beam of the searchlight touched across the boat's path, probing for open water.

'It looks kind of bad,' Mud said. He straightened, gasping for breath, then bent quickly to the capstan-bar.

'If we just get a few yards past the hump.' The skipper stepped to the forward edge of the square bow and for a moment took hold of the wire with his bare hands. 'Then we could hang onto the line and drop anchor and keep the engines running till daybreak.'

'This is suicide, skipper.' Peter looked up at the darkness as a floe thudded against the barge, jarring so hard that the wire slipped on the capstan-head.

'She's going to be a close shave,' Pottle said. 'That is one dandy big ice-cube. Mother of God, if we just had a bottle that would do it justice.'

The main pan of ice came down and hit the port side of the barge, not like the candled ice of spring, rotten and green, but new and clear and hard as glass.

'It'll go over the hump and break up fast,' the skipper said.

'I think we can hold,' Louttit said, his face a blank in the circle of scarf.

The ice hit the front of the barge's shovel-nosed bow and seemed to hesitate. Then the barge began to move. It moved to the starboard toward the rock.

'Just hold your breath,' the skipper said. 'It'll turn and be free. Then the river is all ours.'

'We got bad luck aboard,' Pottle said.

They could hear ice sawing at the wood. A deckhand spoke in the darkness. 'She's taking a good deal of water, skipper. I can hear it now.'

'She's been taking water all day.'

'But it sounds worse now.' The speaker was Louttit. 'Like we sprung a leak. Maybe the oakum —'

The skipper went to a well and listened and swore. 'Slack off on that wire a little.'

The men with the capstan-bars eased up and Pottle let some slack into the wire by loosening the turns on the head of the capstan. But the barge didn't move when the wire went slack.

'Jesus H.,' the skipper said. 'Mud, run back and tell Jonas to cut her to half ahead.'

Mud, awkward on the slippery deck, left running, his capstan-bar clattering onto the deck behind him. 'Go slow', Pottle called, 'so the flies can keep up.' Perceptibly now the barge began to tilt, the starboard side going up, the port almost level with the water.

'We're hard aground,' Peter said. 'On the rock.'

'Let go the wire. Jump to it, mate.'

Pottle tossed the coils of wire off the capstan. Still the barge didn't move. The ice on the port side cracked loudly and a new edge of ice jarred up and slid over the broken-off fragment and came at the barge as if alive. Suddenly the bow end of the barge twisted, the port side corner going under the water and ice; timbers cracked and a knuckle-board splintered.

'Run for it,' the skipper shouted. 'On the high side, for Jesus' sake. For your bloody lives.'

They scrambled in a confused heap up along the creaking and rising deck, stepping on each other, kicking each other in their haste and the darkness and then bracing themselves with their hands and feet between the rising deck and the tilting wall of the deck-house, and then groping on all fours. The *Nahanni Jane's* engines were suddenly cut to half speed. The barge began to swing, pivoting on the rock.

'I can't swim!' Abraham was shouting from the invisible bow. 'I can't. I can't swim!'

Peter stopped and waited. 'Billy?'

'I can't swim, for God's sake!'

Peter turned and dropped back over the corner of the deck-house and into the darkness. Abraham was clinging to a chock where he had almost climbed overboard; his feet dangled off into the blackness over the water and ice.

Peter grabbed a handful of shirt and pulled mightily.

Abraham came up and caught hold of Peter's belt and held on as Peter slipped climbing and then fell against the deck-house wall. 'We'll all be dead. We'll all be like that corpse back there grey from the water and nobody will drag the river. Who the hell would get us — '

Peter gave him a shove forward.

They scrambled through the darkness and found the bow of the boat. Someone was calling. Cursing and calling. The searchlight came down and blinded them and then left and they groped in the stunning blackness; they found the guardrail on the boat's bow and tumbled aboard as a breaking line whipped behind them. Abraham fell onto deck and clutched his knee.

The barge was breaking in half. On the port side of the swinging barge the wooden house was crumpling like paper, the hogposts spilling out of line.

'That other ratchet!' the skipper ordered.

Louttit picked up a sledge and hit the ratchet, broke the pelican hook; the wire snaked away and the barge was free.

Arnafson came running forward from the darkness behind

a deck light. 'Everybody here?' He reached and touched the men one by one.

'We're all okay,' the skipper said. He looked around again. 'You okay, Abraham?'

'Just ticked me.' He sat on the deck rubbing his knee. 'A breaking line can cut you in half.'

The *Nahanni Jane* was falling back now. They watched as the barge turned onto its side and began to drift free of the rock, pushed by the ice. The barge broke in half, dumping bright yellow machines like toys into the ice and the dark water.

'There's no bottom here,' the mate said. 'Here in the chute.'

Peter tried to help Abraham up but he wouldn't move. He went on rubbing his knee. 'If we took as good care of ourselves as we take of the corpse, we'd all live forever.'

The skipper stopped on his way up to the pilot-house. 'You boys move that thing off the stern. I don't want to hear any more whimpering. A dead man is just a dead man.'

'Didn't you hear what that woman said last night?' Pottle bent and helped Abraham to his feet. 'Or are we going to go on pretending she didn't say anything?'

Peter turned back from looking out at the black water and the shattering pan of ice. He started toward the galley, unable again to approach Kettle's door.

'Bad luck doesn't just happen,' Pottle said. 'We've got a right to ask a few questions. What in hell did that woman mean?'

'There'll be people asking enough questions. Enough and some more.' The skipper's voice came out of the darkness in front of the pilot-house. 'Guy, you looked for the body day and night. You were more anxious than the rest of us to get it back. Go show the boys what you want done.'

Angi Boyle was standing at the rail in front of the galley door, smoking a cigarette and ignoring the fall of snow. Cold as it was, she wouldn't let anyone into the galley for another five minutes. 'At five-thirty,' she said. The crew, behind Peter, crowded to the door as he walked by. 'I can see that canoe when I stand by my stove.' Angi went on. 'Whenever I look up at the clock, I see out a port-hole instead. Why can't you move one little canoe instead of spending all day to sink a barge?'

Mud took a step toward the stern, then saw Peter coming back and stopped. 'He must be froze hard as a rock by now.'

'Catch a death of a cold,' Abraham said. Fat and puffing, he walked bent over and kept on rubbing his knee.

One of the two narrow doors to the galley was open and Pottle stopped in the light. 'Well, Mr. Guy. What do you want us to do? Say a few prayers?'

'Or send for a judge?' Abraham said.

Angi shivered and pulled her sweater closed over her large breasts. 'You ought to show a little consideration for the poor widow. She can see that thing from her back window.'

'Changing her tune all of a sudden, ain't she now?' Pottle grinned. 'Wasn't so full of grief before, was she?'

Angi blew smoke at the tip of her cigarette. Her breath frosted in the cold air.

'Right, Angi? Was she now?'

'I ain't a tattle-tale.'

'Some shocking kind of a widow,' Pottle insisted. 'Might have been a little too anxious to wear the black. If she'd ever bothered to put it on.'

'We could put it out on the barge,' Louttit suggested.

'Ought to put Guy under lock and key in the reefer out there. Nothing in it now but a little ham and some turkeys.' Abraham stopped rubbing at his knee. 'I couldn't sleep a wink with that thing aboard last night.'

'Then you were wide awake and snoring,' Louttit said.

'You've got three minutes till supper.' Angi turned and ducked down into the galley, the cigarette in her mouth, her hands disappearing last, from the overhead bar. 'And I made your favourite dessert,' she called back.

'Rice pudding again,' Mud said. 'After we worked like slaves all day.'

'Only seven nights this week,' Louttit said. 'No whimpering out of you.'

They moved away from the light by the galley door and Peter led the way into the darkness and the falling snow. Louttit pulled the small tarpaulin off the washing-machine that sat on top of the galley beside the lifeboat. He started to cover the inside of the canoe but Peter bent first to shake the snow off the quilt. And straightened with a jerk: 'Whose idea of a joke is this?'

The head of a lamp lay in the canoe beside the covered body. There was no bulb in the lamp. The cord had been ripped off. Everyone bent low over the dim light from the galley port-hole beside their feet, looking at the bald lamp head, and Peter was picking it up when a voice spoke:

'She was out here, this afternoon.'

Abraham started back with a jump.

'Fooling around, Jonas just told me.' The skipper came out of the darkness. 'While the rest of us were out on the barge — ' He looked hard at the lamp in Peter's hand. 'What you got there?'

'It was in the canoe.'

'It was like hell in the canoe. It's the one we found dragging the river.'

'But it was — '

McAlpine fell to his knees beside the canoe and fumbled and found the end of the cord and touched it to the lamp. 'I'll be damned.' He tried the cord and the lamp again, disbelieving, wanting to disbelieve. 'Well I'll be damned. Jonas said she came out here. With something in her hands. And then she went running away.'

Pottle was squatted down, shaking his head. 'When he was drowning and fighting — he must have tore it loose.'

'You should have stopped him,' Mud burst out. 'You shouldn't have let him jump, Pete.'

Peter stepped away from the canoe and the others straightened and stepped back and the canoe was left alone in the pale light and the falling snow.

'But he was done for anyhow. He died faster that way.' Peter raised his hands in a gesture of resignation.

'You'd like to think so,' Abraham said. 'You struck out to save your own hide. You'd like to think you were doing him a favour. When you high-tailed off that barge.'

'He was burned black. Somebody saw him. Kartuk saw —'

'You're weak on witnesses,' the skipper said. 'Or would you like me to call out the cook?'

'She doesn't know what she saw.'

'She didn't have her back to the scene. She was emptying a bowl of carrots and saw the whole shebang.'

'But the last time she told it he was wearing a hat. He didn't have a hat. I wouldn't trust anything —'

'I guess you wouldn't, Mr. Guy. I guess you'd just as soon we asked Hornyak here.'

Peter looked around at the blackness of water and cliff. He could drop the lamp here; throw it overboard and after the splash he could assure them all they were spotless as lambs. He spoke to the skipper:

'Do you wish him alive?'

'I like him the way he is.'

'Did you wish him dead?'

'I wished the bastard dead in his grave.'

'That's what I mean.'

'But I didn't put him there.'

'Not you, skipper. It wasn't McAlpine's job to see that the barge was cleaned. He's just the skipper. Right? It wasn't the chief's job to look after the equipment for doing the job. Hell no. It wasn't Pottle's job to be out there supervising. He isn't the mate, is he? It wasn't the deckhands' job to be down there inside to do the cleaning. Was it now? Was it, skipper? Would he be dead if we'd done our jobs?'

'By the way, Guy,' McAlpine said. 'Do you wish him alive?'

Peter didn't answer.

'If you wished him alive, why did you give him that light, Guy?'

'He asked for it,' Peter said.

'Did he ask for a lamp that had no shield?'

'He was born lucky, that lucky bastard.'

'And look at the lucky bastard,' the skipper said. 'How long you been on these boats, Guy?'

'Long enough to know who's responsible for what.'

'And long enough to know you shouldn't stop him from jumping, you coward, because if you had he might be alive this minute. Or would he have too much to say? If he'd lived for half an hour, even. Would he still have had too much to say? About his wife and our fine Mr. Guy?'

McAlpine waited and Peter didn't speak.

'About how he knew Mr. Guy years ago. How, like the cook says, they argued over the dinner-table the first minute they met. But I'll let you give your alibi when we get to Norman Wells.' McAlpine signalled. 'Come on, boys. We've got to get this boat tied up.'

The *Nahanni Jane* coasted up beside *Barge 301* and the deckhands ran at the skipper's order, someone to make the bow fast, someone to find a stern line, someone to set a check line. The skipper went forward to climb to the pilot-house and the stern deck was left deserted except for the canoe and Peter.

He bent to cover the corpse with the tarpaulin. Just once, before he put down the tarpaulin, he dared raise the quilt; in the queer light from the galley port-hole he saw only a shadow and could not make out the face. In his hurry to cover it over again his hand brushed a frozen arm. He looked around to see that no one was watching; with a quick gesture he moved and dropped the lamp over the stern, into the dark water.

The whole crew had somehow come to assume that the body was Peter's. And after the first shock, the first impulse to deny, he found the idea not really an unpleasant one. A vague pride took hold of him; they had given him their guilt and he would keep and claim it, and they could condemn him if so they pleased.

Only in the morning it was he who took them through the rapids. Jonas quit, in spirit and in body. He came listlessly to breakfast and told the skipper he had an upset stomach, from powdered potatoes, he guessed, and he asked permission to go back to bed. And when the skipper said no he went anyhow.

It was Peter who took the boat up over the hump to where they could pick up the line they had laid the previous day and the end of which they had lost last evening. After they picked up the line he dropped the boat back and buoyed the end of the line and went into the canyon for the last barge and came up again and hooked onto the line, and in three hours, with some hard winching, and with Peter at the wheel looking for easy water, taking every advantage in the current, working so close to the rock that a man could have jumped onto it from the boat, they got the boat and barge through. The skipper paced the deck, silently and aimlessly.

They unhooked the line from the deadman and picked up *Barge 309* and they were away, Peter standing Jonas's watch and his own, the skipper or a deckhand taking the wheel for an hour or two on an easy stretch of river. Peter took them through the Sans Sault Rapids. He kept them travelling all night and all the next day and into the night again.

He did it without Jonas. Old Jonas would not come up to the pilot-house. Now and then he appeared on the bow or at a rail and watched the water and the shore and the sky for a while, his curved pipe empty in his mouth. He was old, his hands arthritic and his eyesight failing now. Peter must do it alone; without the man who taught him as much about the river as the river itself had taught him. For his teacher was old Jonas Bird, an Indian who was pleased that a white man should want to know a wind spot from a rock riffle, a boil spot from a hidden boulder; that a college man should want to know what a flock of ducks could tell him about the depth of water, what rising fish could tell him about the current. He did not ask why Peter wanted to know but patiently taught him how to get through the Sans Sault and the Green Island rapids, where to relay heavy barges on the Blackwater stretch, how to run through the Providence Rapids while looking at a distant hill and making a critical turn when a moment's miscalculation could mean a barge stove in. Jonas taught him, quiet withdrawn Jonas, unwilling to speak to anyone outside the pilot-house, who in his youth made a love potion to win a wife and won her and then lost his first son by killing a wolf, who wore a crucifix and a medicine-bag on a string around his neck and one winter drove a dog-team six hundred miles to get vaccine to stop an epidemic. Who each spring knew when the ice would go out.

It was Jonas who taught him a pilot's first lesson: you must learn how to go down a river, and then you must learn how to come back up. That was the first thing Jonas taught him.

And now they were approaching Norman Wells.

Ahead and above the horizon he could see the fixed red aircraft warning lights on the two radio masts. The last time he landed here, at this same hour, the sun was shining; now only the Northern Lights flickered and played across a dark sky, sending long shadows into the river from the shore, deceptive shadows that confused a pilot into thinking the river was narrowing and would disappear as he watched.

And the last time he left here he had not wanted to go so soon; he wanted to continue the dragging operation, the search for Michael Hornyak's body. Just one more hour, he asked.

Now they had Hornyak's body. It had floated a hundred miles before it snagged on a deadhead and was finally exposed by the falling water. Now they had it. As if by dragging five hundred miles downriver and back again he had found it himself and was bringing it ashore.

It lay out there in front of him, in the reefer on *Barge 301* where he had put it, canoe and all, with a little help from Mud and Louttit. He was bringing it back.

And here he was supposed to put Kettle Hornyak on a plane. For Fraser's sake as well as for Kettle's, he was supposed to see her safely aboard, on a plane that was going south. Safely out of the country. Safely back to civilization. For his own sake too? he wondered.

The waves turned silver away from the bow of the forward barge, a single wave on either side. Behind him the boat trailed a fluorescent tail. The shores were dark and one with their deep-flung shadows. The *Nahanni Jane* was, according to the radio skeds, the last boat on the river. For all others the season was over; they were out of the water and up on the ways.

And he could end his season here too. If Jonas would come up and take the wheel. He could himself fly out with the body if not with Kettle. But now the responsibility of piloting was all his and the skipper kept coming into the pilot-house and muttering about a boat to deliver to Yellowknife. So a bunch of carpenters and welders could go to work and turn her into a fish-packer by spring.

He began the crossing toward the far side of the river and the pier. The wheel moved easily in his hands, the chains creaking below his feet in the darkness. He kept the wheel-house lights turned off so he could better see the river. Only the running lights were burning, red and green on top of the wheelhouse, and below and behind him light from the galley and engine-room port-holes just faintly streaked the water. Around him was darkness, yet far across the river he could see snow on the low Franklin Mountains: now in the night he could see better than he had been able to see on their day of departure.

I could leave on the plane, he thought. But am I damned now to follow her around, like Mud taking her coffee and passing her everything but the galley stove at the table and blushing at the mention of her name? At least Hornyak somehow remained free. If he was free with that woman. If not having kids when he wanted them could be called freedom. Kids and a future and a past. Maybe Hornyak had his moments too when he pleaded and was shouted away or was smiled under the table. Like himself now, afraid to go to the bloody john for fear he'd see that woman outside the cook's cabin door. Afraid to walk into his own cabin for fear she'd be there, reading a book, curled up in his sleeping-bag. His guts gone to jelly and still all of him hoping she'd be there; his looking out back not to check the boat's wash but just hoping to catch a glimpse of her as she ducked into the galley for a bite to eat.

At least on the river he had the dignity of his skill. He was a pilot. He was one of a handful of men who knew this river. And they delivered supplies to the far end whether men like Fraser knew it was necessary or not. They were that thin but necessary tie. You could send a wire to Vancouver for another skipper or mate or chief. But you had to find your pilots here; they had to have this river in their heads.

A white river bum with a river in his head to keep everything else out.

He glanced down at the reefer on *Barge 301* as if this time to give the indestructible answer. The reefer sat square and ominous and grey on a deck that had once been painted red. On the stern of the barge were mounted a motor and pump for pumping off. Down the centre were three sets of air vents, eight feet high, like black chimneys from which the houses had been removed. On the bow were a capstan and a coil of wire and a gangplank. There was frost on the red bow. And to the left and slightly behind the capstan was the man-hole from which Hornyak had crawled, had kept on crawling, even after his clothes were burnt to ashes and his skin was fried and his hair set straight on end and singed almost to his skull. But he kept on climbing, with the skin hanging off his fingers and sticking to the steel rungs, and he climbed out and walked to the bow of the barge and jumped.

My God, and what if he drowned himself? What if, even then, he was still master? If he recognized his predicament and dealt with that too. 'No. No —'

'Something the matter up there?'
'I was just singing to myself.'
'Sounded like a bloody foghorn.'
The voice was silent on the deck below him. Peter assumed a deckhand was bringing him coffee. He leaned forward through the window to see who it was. Then he could make out three or four figures on the deck. They were apparently waiting for their eyes to adjust to the dark.
'What's up?' Peter called.
'Is that Norman Wells over there?'
'Half an hour, and you can get your feet muddy.'
'We've got some ideas,' the voice answered. It was Pottle's.
The men came up the ladder and into the dark pilot-house. There were three of them. They gathered behind Peter as if he was about to shoot a rapids. A mile and a half of smooth water lay between them and the shore. The skipper spoke first: 'I think maybe we ought to keep running.'
'Running?' The word slapped Peter into awareness.
'Right on through. I checked with all the crew. They're game to go on short supplies.'
'There's plenty to eat,' Pottle said.
'If you like turkey,' Abraham said.
'We can pick up a few things at The Wells,' Peter suggested.
The skipper oozed a little impatience into his voice. 'But that's it. It'll be six hours before anybody's stirring on land. That'll be six hours shot right there.'
'And this clear weather,' Pottle said, 'It won't last for ever.'
'Don't we have to load oil?'
'The head office radios to keep highballing. They need those two barges on the lake for spring traffic.'
Peter studied the approaching shore. A single flame burned down on the beach; waste from the refinery. Now he could

just dimly make out a row of oil-tanks on the bank. It was true; no one would be available until eight or eight-thirty, even to sell them some cold-storage eggs and a couple of quarters of beef.

'We've been talking to Jonas,' the skipper said. 'He's starting to feel a little better. He says if we land he goes ashore but if we keep going he'll be feeling his oats in a day or two.'

'I've been thinking I might go ashore myself,' Peter said.

The skipper grunted and stepped forward to the window on the opposite side of the wheel from Peter. 'We got to deliver this outfit to Yellowknife. You know that yourself, Pete.'

'I thought I had some questions to answer. Police.'

'I cleared everything last night on radio sked.'

'Then how about the body?'

There was no immediate answer. Ahead of them the shore loomed larger. Peter could make out now the end of the pier, a darker shadow against the shimmer of the Northern Lights on a streak of faster-flowing water. They were coming now into the area where they spent three days dragging.

'Guy, we can't stop.' Pottle scratched his head vigorously in the darkness. 'You ought to understand that, Guy.'

'You ought to be the first to understand,' the skipper said. 'At Yellowknife it'll be different.'

'While here at The Wells' — Pottle stepped up beside Peter as if to wrest the wheel from him — 'there'll be a lot of questions asked. And we know what happened. It wasn't your fault any more than it was anybody else's. So why waste more time filling out more forms for some ass up there in some office?'

'Did you tell them on your radio sked that you're bringing in the body?'

The skipper cracked two knuckles on one hand. 'I didn't think I'd bother them till we knew what time we'd get here.'

'They don't even know that the body's been found?'

'Not yet, really. It didn't seem necessary yet.'

'Well why don't you dump it overboard?'

'Christ, Guy, we've got nothing to hide. Have you got something to hide? I'm only suggesting we take the body to Yellow-knife where it will have to go anyhow. This good weather won't last forever.'

'You're afraid.' Peter turned and tried to see the faces around him in the darkness: castaways, exiles, fugitives. But he saw only the silhouettes of uneasy and vaguely worried men. The skipper avoiding a dull marriage. Pottle who had been saying for as long as anyone could remember that he was on his way back to Newfoundland but who never got there. Abra-ham who wouldn't go outside at all because he was half Indi-an and would end up living in a ghetto. 'You're all afraid,' he said. 'You're afraid to take this body ashore. You're afraid to get rid of it and you're afraid to keep it. They won't hang all of you, for Christ sake. They won't hang any of you. Maybe they'll hang me. But I'm ready to risk it.'

'Nobody's going to hang for anything,' the skipper said soft-ly. 'There has to be a crime before you start hanging people. We just want to do what's right. We want to see that justice is done, Guy, and not an injustice. We've got principles too you know. You didn't invent the damned things.'

Peter began to move the wheel slowly, bringing the boat in-to position for a landing. 'I say if we don't stop — take the skiff and let Pottle and a couple of deckhands tow the body ashore. I don't care if they just leave it on the dock and run.'

'You won't catch me in that skiff,' Abraham said.

'Where're Louttit and Mud?' Peter said.

'They said they want to sleep. But they agreed.'

'And the chief?'

'He took over the engines so the second can check the fuel.'

Peter noticed now for the first time a shadowy figure mov-ing slowly about on the deck below him. The second engineer was measuring the tanks, rubbing chalk onto a long stick and dropping it into the boat's tanks and raising it.

'We've got lots of fuel,' the skipper said. 'But we just wanted to make sure.'

Peter watched the shadow on deck as it attempted to read

the dipstick without a light. 'He's an odd duck,' Peter said. 'What did he say?'

'We didn't bother to check,' Pottle said. 'I can't tell if that bugger's alive or dead.'

'Don't ask me where the head office found him.' The skipper was cracking his knuckles again. 'They just put him on a plane and sent him in. But the chief says he knows his job.'

'I ain't heard him speak a word yet,' Abraham said.

'You ought to follow his example,' Peter said.

The shadow climbed onto the first barge, limping, and went out to sound the bunker compartments. It walked around past the reefer and disappeared.

'We're getting in close,' Peter said. 'Look, I'll take the corpse in myself. And Mrs. Hornyak.'

The skipper gently put a hand on the wheel. 'We need two pilots, Guy. Jonas isn't up to it. It's a long haul yet. The Blackwater. And Green Island and Providence. We'll have to relay the barges.'

'You sons of bitches. You're kidnapping me.'

'Guy, we're crowded for time.'

'But in half an hour even, you can dump the corpse off. And me with it.'

'We'll be saving you a lot of grief,' the skipper said. 'You're your own worst enemy, by God. You can deliver your corpse to Yellowknife, and then you can catch a flight out the same day.'

'*My* corpse. I don't want to take my corpse to Yellowknife. I want to leave it right here.'

'We're running straight on through,' the skipper said. 'You will be thankful later.'

'And how about Mrs. Hornyak? I suppose you'll send her ashore in the skiff with her baggage and dump her on the beach.'

'No.' The skipper tapped the wheel. 'Jesus, Guy, you can be thick-headed. She's got some misconceptions that I think one of us should explain. Like maybe me or you. In fact why

I came up here. I was sure you'd see our point. But I wondered if you could maybe run down and go tell her? It'll be a few days before we put her ashore. Skipper's orders.'

Peter held the wheel steady; he could feel the first tug on the rudders of the stronger current off the end of the pier. 'You know something, skipper? I'm up here in this wheelhouse alone for most of the day. And there's a two-way radio hanging right back of me there on the wall.'

The skipper let himself chuckle softly. 'I've got confidence, Mr. Guy. A good skipper has confidence in his crew. All the confidence in the world.'

He stopped in front of Kettle's door and looked out at the river and hesitated. Here he sought Hornyak's body. Here he dragged back and forth across the current, the prongs of the dragging-hooks ticking the gravel bottom and sending shocks up into his arm, and after awhile the fear turned to something comforting. He knocked softly and listened and then knocked softly again.

There was no answer and he stood watching; out in the river on the two islands, Bear and Goose, the trees had shed their yellow leaves; the evergreens were black against the dark sky. And the boat was swinging into the main channel.

He knocked again, harder this time.

'Yes?' a voice answered, struggling out of sleep.

'It's me. Peter.'

'Yes?'

'I've got to talk to you for a minute.'

And again sleepily: 'Mike?'

'Kettle! Kettle! It's me. Pete.'

But quickly: 'Stay out.' And after a moment, 'Stay out,' again.

He opened the door slowly and stepped up carefully into the dark cabin and let the door swing shut on his heel. He groped for and found the rail of the top bunk and leaned to where Kettle's head must be. It was darker in here than outside. The cook was snoring slightly in the lower bunk; she shifted or turned and stopped snoring but went on breathing heavily. He bent close over the bunk and Kettle was breathing regularly; he couldn't tell if she was asleep or waiting.

'Kettle?'

'Yes.'

'We're here. We're at Norman Wells.'

'Peter?' She moved on the pillow. 'Is it time for breakfast?'

'It's some time after two.'

'The cook said we'd be there for breakfast. I'm all packed.' Her voice was muffled in the blanket again.

'We're not going to tie up. We're not going to land.' Groping, he accidentally touched her hair, but didn't move his fingers. 'We're going to keep running.'

'Running?' Her head turned and her face came out of the blanket.

'I mean — you know. Running. Going. We aren't stopping. The skipper says we won't stop.'

'Running?' she repeated. 'Peter?'

'Day and night,' Peter said. 'We've been running day and night. We're making good time.'

'Where've you been, Peter?'

'I've been standing here trying to wake you. I've been at the bloody wheel till I can't see.'

'I was dreaming.' She reached out and caught his arm, her grip hard, frightened. Then she let go and rubbed at her eyes and huddled down under the blankets. 'It's cold again. It's always cold. The only warm place is in bed. But I keep dreaming.'

Peter didn't know how to begin again. 'Kettle. Did you hear what I said at first?'

'We're running, you said.'

'We're not going to stop at The Wells.'

Kettle was awake now. 'We've got to stop at The Wells.'

'We're there right now. We're going by.'

Kettle raised up on an elbow. 'Are you here, Peter?' She reached out and touched him. 'They forgot to put me off.'

'Kettle, for God's sake, the skipper won't let you off. He won't let anybody go ashore.'

Kettle was silent. Then: 'What about —'

'Mike?'

'Yes.'

'Not him either.'

'But they hate him. They all hate his body. You see it on their faces. Why don't they get rid of him?'

'They're keeping him too. For the police in Yellowknife.'

She stirred in the bunk. 'That's not why.'

He could see the white of her pajamas but no head above. 'Why then?'

'They're all deathly afraid.'

'I know.'

'Why are they all afraid, Pete?'

'I'm not sure.'

'Are you afraid, Pete?'

'I keep wondering. I don't know.'

'I have dreams. I was dreaming. I keep dreaming he's alive and at the same time I know he's dead and there he is alive. And I go to touch him and I don't touch anything. I keep dreaming it over and over. He's sitting in the car beside me, driving, and I know he's dead. And I go to touch him.'

'Don't tell me,' he said.

'I won't go without the body.'

'But that's it. They won't let you go.'

'I'll go if I please. They can't keep me, Peter.'

'Standing outside, I was wondering.' He moved his head closer to hers and whispered lower. 'Can you row a boat?'

'I grew up on this river.'

'We could drop the skiff over and put you in and cut you

loose. If you can row you'll be ashore in twenty minutes. Just drift, and row a little to the right. There's a flame on the shore. Try and land above the flame.'

'I won't go without the body,' she said.

'Kettle, Christ, you're as bad as the rest of them.'

'Are you going?'

He shook his head in the darkness. 'No. For good or bad, I'm pilot on this tub. I've got to see the thing through.'

'You're staying for him, aren't you? Not for the boat at all.'

'I don't know,' Peter said. 'I'm staying.'

'I'm going outside. Away from this awful country and all its crazy people.'

'And what'll you do till you come back?'

'I'll never come back. I'll find a sensible man. You two have been crazy. And I'll have kids and take them for rides in the country and take them to movies. When I'm awake that's all I think about. Taking the kids into the country and to see movies. And I'll teach them to grow up like civilized people.'

'Good for you, Kettle.'

'God, Mike — '

'Peter,' he said. *'Pete — '*

'Peter, don't be sarcastic, all I've got to do here is think. I can't even talk to that cook any more. She keeps saying don't worry. Over and over — ' Then she remembered and held her breath until she heard the cook's heavy breathing. 'I think about everything Dad tried to say. About being civilized or making a mess — '

'But I've been wanting to talk to you,' Peter said. 'I went for drives in the country. I went to the movies. Serials that never ended and every Saturday we all took our money and lined up to find out what never ended.'

'Even that night, Peter, in the mountains. From then on it was all cockeyed somehow. You know. I was married eight days after I met him. After I knew you two years. I didn't even know his middle initial. I don't know it yet.'

'He had his initials on a tie clip,' Peter said. 'But one night

111

in a little town in Alberta he gave it to a girl who said she wanted something to remember him by. He gave her his initials.'

'But he gave me everything. He just spent money and bought me what I wanted. And one day he flew into a rage because I didn't want anything. Because I didn't *want* anything, Pete. And then I got mad and said I wanted lots of things. Like what, he said. Well, like — And I couldn't tell him, Peter. And he got mad and yelled, for Christ sake, what, woman? Tell me for Christ sake. And then he laughed and kissed me and I wanted to cry and he wouldn't let me, he made me laugh. You understand, Peter? I wanted to ask for something that would smash him. Part of me wanted to. Something that would break him. Something that would crush him right there. And all the time something else inside me was protecting him and I couldn't think of anything and he laughed and said I'm it, young lady. I'm what you wanted. And in three days we were married.'

'But they won't put him ashore,' Peter said. 'That's one thing he can't have.' He found and held the rail of her bunk with both hands as if he expected a great explosion. 'There's one thing he can't do, he can't go ashore right now. They've got him and they're not going to let go.'

She lay back and covered herself with the blankets. 'I don't want to go ashore. Do you mind, Peter?'

'I'm glad,' he said. He groped for the door. 'I've got to get back to the wheel.'

'Peter?' she called.

He was closing the door. His heart raced. 'Yes?'

'Who did it, Peter? Who killed him? For God's sake tell me. I don't want to dream.'

'I don't know,' Peter whispered. 'I don't know. I've been wondering. That's what I wanted to ask you about.' He waited and she said nothing. 'But I've got to go take the wheel.'

At first they ate turkey and canned ham and smoked ham and then turkey and canned ham and now they ate turkey. For five days they had eaten turkey. For dinner and supper and between-meal snacks. They only rebelled now when Angi offered them a heaped platter of cold turkey for breakfast.

'I don't mind eating the stuff,' Pottle said. 'It's these feathers I'm sprouting. They make me sneeze.'

'They get in the way when I sit down,' Arnafson said. 'If we don't leave here today I'm taking the bunk out of my cabin and putting in a roost.'

Peter stepped over the green bench and sat down and turned up his plate and cup. 'Maybe we can fly out in a day or two. If the wind holds, and we don't start moulting.'

They had been windbound for six days behind Lobstick Island. They had got to the river's outlet in seven days of hard pushing. All the way upstream, against rapids and boulders and sandbars and the floes of ice that were running out of Beaver Lake. And then, before them, lay Great Slave Lake. And for six days more they had looked day and night at the pounding, white-capped waves.

Arnafson had been drinking all night, by himself, and for the moment was in a jovial mood. 'I like turkey,' he said. 'I always liked turkey. I like turkey for Christmas and turkey for Thanksgiving. Why not like turkey for breakfast?'

'Have some,' the cook said.

'No, thank you,' Arnafson said.

He picked up the platter of turkey and stared closely at the slices of white and dark meat, at the wings and drumsticks, the beak of his cap brushing a bone. 'Cook, you should give prizes. You should hide shots of rum in your cold turkey.'

The skipper clattered down the three steps into the galley and came to the table. 'Is everybody here?'

'We're going to try it!' Pottle said. 'Steak for breakfast in Yellowknife tomorrow! Bloody red steak and a case of Bohemian Maid.'

'Not quite,' McAlpine said. His hair was mussed and he hadn't put on a shirt over his long underwear. He hadn't shaved in a few days now. 'Is that woman still in your cabin, Angi?'

'You ought to know the answer, skipper,' the chief interrupted. 'Try to be patient till you get to Yellowknife.'

'She is indeed.' Angi snatched the platter of turkey out of Arnafson's hands. 'She's part of the furniture. She's grown to her bunk. And I'm here too, in case nobody has noticed lately.'

'Who hasn't showed up for chow?'

The men looked around the table at each other. Pottle set down the plate of powdered eggs. Mud was left holding the plate of toast he was offering to Louttit.

'The skiff is gone.'

'The hell you say,' Pottle said.

'Abraham,' Louttit said. 'His bunk was empty this morning. But he was supposed to be on watch.'

'Well he isn't,' McAlpine said. 'I've been all over the boat looking. And Jonas isn't in his cabin.'

'He hasn't been to breakfast,' the cook said. 'But here lately he's been sleeping in.'

'The dirty thieving bums,' Pottle said.

'I hope no turkey's missing,' Angi said. 'I was planning roast turkey for dinner.'

'Well you'll have two less to feed.'

'Last night,' Louttit raised a forkful of powdered eggs, 'last night after supper Jonas said we can't possibly make it. It's too late in the season, he said.'

'If this wind would let up.' The skipper felt his whiskers. He went to a port-hole and looked out at the half light. 'I could take this outfit across the lake with a good kicker.'

Louttit put down his forkful of eggs. 'Last night he said we're getting too jumpy. We'll do something foolish, he said.'

'How come you know so much?' the skipper said.

'He was talking. He never talks, so I listened.'

'You mean – they asked you to go along.'

'Well I'm here, ain't I? And I've been here for six days. Like everybody else. So if I had a chance to leave and missed it, I'm a bigger fool than the rest of you.' Louttit pulled out a red handkerchief and mopped his forehead.

'I wish they'd asked me,' Arnafson said. 'Didn't they need a good engineer?'

'We could go back to Providence and find them,' the skipper said. 'They'd have to head for Providence.'

'And you'd spend all winter looking,' Louttit said. 'They'd be into the bush the minute they saw our stack. You might find their tracks by spring if you were lucky.'

'We should follow their lead instead of their tracks,' Arnafson said. 'We could take this outfit back to Horn River to freeze in. The N. T. boats do it all the time. We could take the lifeboat and kicker up to Fort Providence from there and radio for a plane to pick us up.'

'With a hundred and sixty miles to go?' The skipper half laughed and half scoffed. 'After coming clear from the coast?'

'And only losing one barge,' Arnafson said. 'That should tickle the head office to death.'

'That was it,' Louttit said. 'Jonas blamed himself. Except sometimes he blamed it on that body.'

'He was right the second time,' Arnafson said.

'Where'd you get the booze?' McAlpine said.

'I've been saving two bottles. Ever since the explosion. Good old overproof rum for when we get to Yellowknife. Only we aren't going to get there.'

'Not without an engineer, we won't,' the skipper said.

'Not with one. Because Hornyak is getting his due from us. He interrupted a perfectly good drunk back at The Wells. And he's still interrupting. He has interrupted us right onto the lee side of this stinking little island where we're going to freeze in.'

'Jonas had bad eyes and he was getting scared to run at night.'

'And he was a living bloody weather-vane.' The chief stood up slowly. 'If you'll excuse me. I must get to my cabin. Because I ain't going to get anywhere else today.' He staggered out of the galley, up the steps; he was laughing to himself as he went and laughter trailed off behind him into the silent galley.

'I wish he'd pass it around.' Angi began dropping hotcake batter into a frying-pan. 'Once in a while he takes a nip down to the second, but the rest of us might as well be teetotallers.'

'What's the forecast?' Pottle said. 'It can't blow forever, can it? I'm dry as a wooden gun.'

'Less wind today.'

'That's what it said yesterday.'

'And the day before,' Angi said. 'They play a record. It's top on the Hit Parade.'

116

McAlpine sat down where the chief had been sitting and the cook gave him a clean plate and cup and offered him the turkey. 'Have some of the bacon you picked up at The Wells while I was sound asleep.' He waved the turkey away. The table was half covered with tins of strawberry jam and marmalade, a sugar-bowl and a tin of milk, two kinds of pickles, syrup, mustard, salt, pepper, honey in a paper container, peanut butter, HP sauce, ketchup. 'Is there anything to eat?'

Mud handed him the powdered eggs.

'Jonas,' Louttit said. 'He was windbound here one time for fifteen days. He lost two hundred dollars playing rummy.'

'I've lost four dollars myself,' Mud said, 'on that cribbage board. Plus all those new rubbers I paid five dollars to get in Aklavik.'

'Shame on you, young man,' Angi said. 'It serves you right.'

'Abraham was winning everything,' Pottle said. 'I don't see why he skinned out.'

Louttit put down his coffee cup. 'Those rubbers weren't doing him any good here.'

'He could send up rescue signals,' Peter said, 'or weather balloons.'

'Or maybe go see the widow,' McAlpine said, 'since our pilot seems to be falling down on the job.'

'There's enough wind in here,' Angi said, 'to keep us windbound for another six days.' She stacked more hotcakes onto Mud's plate.

The skipper had his mouth full of eggs. 'Our pilot here keeps going up to the wheelhouse and looking through the binoculars and shaking his head.'

Pottle grinned. 'Afraid you'll get seasick, Guy?'

'Afraid I won't get to Yellowknife at all if we start out now. The *Sandy* went down in weather like this. And she had more horsepower than we've got.'

'I just don't want to die of old age behind Lobstick Island.'

'If we keep throwing turkey bones overboard,' Mud said, 'we'll soon be aground.'

'We'd be wasting our time,' Peter said. 'We were laying in here one time when the *Sickanni Chief* pulled out. Towing two empty barges. The wind took them backwards. In forty minutes they were out on deck chopping ice. And in two hours they were tied up beside us again.'

'A great place to honeymoon,' Angi said. 'While all the bars in Yellowknife go broke and have to close.'

'Maybe Pete would like to skin out like our other pilot,' Pottle said.

'He wasn't skinning out,' Peter said.

'What the hell would you call it?'

'I'd call it old and tired and sick of being nagged into doing something he didn't want to do to begin with. Like taking the wheel when he didn't believe we should be coming up here at all. When we could have had the boat and the barges pulled by now, back at Axe Point.'

'I'd call it no guts myself, Mr. Guy. But I'm sure you've got another name for it.'

'Okay, okay,' McAlpine said. 'We'll wait till tomorrow morning. If the lake isn't any calmer by then — we go back to Horn River.' He hit the bottom of the ketchup bottle with the palm of his hand and ketchup covered his eggs and his coffee cup. He swore at the bottle and banged it down. 'They're going to spill the beans, those bastards, when they get to Providence.' He looked at Pottle. 'So have your pal sobered up and ready to travel.'

Early in the afternoon Arnafson put his fist through the mirror in the washroom; he was trying to drive away his mother from looking at him and calling him a drunkard. Jerry Pottle went in to try and calm him down and Peter went to the galley for the first aid kit to treat the cut hand. Now they had the hand bandaged and the chief was stretched out on his bunk in his cabin, the beak of his engineer's cap pulled close over his eyes. Pottle was trying to take off his shoes and he kicked and fought and whimpered like a child.

118

'He's having the faces,' Pottle said for the fourth or fifth time. 'He sees faces. Drifting in the air or any place. Faces that have no bodies. They accuse him over and over. And he gets to arguing with them and swings at them. Like his parents and brothers and people like that telling him he's a drunkard and no good and all.'

Arnafson began to tremble; then he began to twitch and twist again. He tried to turn over and sit up and Pottle held him down. 'Easy, Bill. Take it easy, b'y. You've got a lot of accusing faces to look at yet before the jig's up.'

'It's the faces,' Pottle continued. 'He sees faces. All by themselves without bodies. And they keep saying he doesn't amount to two cents and why is he good for nothing. Like his mother this time. Only she speaks to him in Icelandic and he can't understand and he gets into a rage. That's why he broke the mirror, trying to drive her off.'

Suddenly Arnafson screamed. It was a high piercing cry of pure fear. He screamed and his body arched up from the bunk.

'Hold his legs so he can't get up,' Pottle said. 'If he gets up we'll both get the whipping of our lives. He's strong as a mule at these times.'

A knock came at the door and then Kettle called: 'My God, isn't there something I can do?'

'Not a damned thing but wait.'

But Kettle opened the door and came in. She was wearing a coat over her pajamas. 'You can hear him all over the boat,' she said. Then she saw his bloody shirt and his bandaged hand. 'It's so quiet everywhere.'

'He sees these faces,' Pottle said.

Arnafson put out a trembling hand and groped for the chair and bottle he had set by his bed; the beak of his cap was still over his eyes.

'You've had enough, b'y.'

'Can't I do something?' Kettle said.

'Get that other shoe, Pete. Then he can't do so much damage kicking.'

119

'Turn off the lights,' Arnafson pleaded.

Peter quickly removed the second shoe.

'The lights,' Arnafson said, his breath beginning to come short. 'So they can't see me. Turn off the lights.'

Then he pushed the cap up off his eyes. His eyes were blood red; his face red and puffed and sweating. He saw Kettle and his eyes widened. 'You!' he shouted.

Kettle backed away and stood against the door.

Arnafson raised his bandaged hand. 'She left me. That one. Forty-nine days was too long for that one.'

'Easy,' Pottle said. 'He sees these faces.'

'That one.' Arnafson went on pointing at Kettle. 'We come off convoy. We come into Halifax and there's nothing in the room. Nobody there after forty-nine days. That two-bit —'

And only a hand over his mouth interrupted the string of obscenities. 'Bill, it's Mrs. Hornyak. There's a lady here in your room.'

'Why did you do it?' Arnafson's anger turned to pleading. 'Why in God's name couldn't you wait?' He turned his swollen eyes to the two men, his bandaged hand still pointing. 'The war wasn't my fault. Make her listen. Just once make her listen.' He flung up both arms as if to protect his face. 'No! It wasn't my fault. I had to go.' He twisted away toward the wall and hid his eyes, the bandaged hand over his head. 'Turn out the lights.'

Pottle took Kettle's arm, gently. 'You better go, Mrs. Hornyak. When he has the faces he does funny things and he's embarrassed if anybody seen him.'

Kettle relented and stepped out of the cabin; Peter saw her look of shock and followed. As he closed the door he heard a stocking foot kick violently against the wall and then a sob and whimpering as of a hurt and lonesome child.

'He sees these faces,' Pottle was explaining helplessly to no one.

'Are you warm enough?' Peter asked Kettle.

They went down the narrow gangplank onto the island; in six days no one had done so except the deckhand who ran ashore briefly with the headline. The island was rocky along the shore, and Kettle was wearing Indian slippers, so they cut inland into the scrub spruce. A fire many years ago had killed the old trees, and a sole tall spruce, stripped of branches nearly to the top, was the lobstick that gave the island its name and served as a marker to boats crossing the lake toward the river's outlet. Among the low trees the moss and lichens were thick and soft and the bushes were stiff and bare of leaves. Berries clustered dead ripe and shrunken, black and red and blue, on stark branches. The sun was shining and in among the low trees and bushes the air was warm and quiet. When they stood still they thought they must hear the frost breaking the few blades of grass. Then, as they listened, holding their breath, they heard a faint stirring of breeze on a twig, a last leaf. And behind that and even softer lay another sound, from the Great Slave side of Lobstick; the chopping of spent waves onto the shore.

They joined hands and walked on and stopped again and walked on. And to hold her hand was a joy more intense than any he could summon into his memory. They had hardly been more than strangers now for days. After the night when they passed Norman Wells they were at first as two people newly introduced. Then there was an awareness of each other that led them to arrive for meals at the same time and to chat together on the stern of the boat while the deck throbbed beneath their feet and the two strips of serrated skyline receded and became one where the river turned. One night Kettle brought him a cup of coffee in the wheelhouse. They were surprised in their casual talk by a deckhand and Kettle quickly found an excuse to leave. For they were both wary. But more so of each other than of the crew. And for the last six days, as the boat lay windbound, they had both, like the crew, slept all night and napped in the morning and the afternoon. They played cribbage together once, with Pottle kibitzing. They dawdled in the galley with the crew and drank coffee and engaged in the endless speculations about the weather.

What seemed to be a path now proved to be only an accidental passageway among the trees. It ended abruptly by becoming a boulder. Kettle laughed. 'Well piloted, oh wise one.'

'Hard aground again,' Peter said. He threw onto some moss the parka he had pulled off as they walked. They sat down and to Kettle's surprise could see beneath the spruce-boughs to a glimpse of the water beyond. She sat and looked out at the water and he lay back with his hands under his head.

'Don't you want to see?' Kettle said. She patted the boulder, suggesting he prop himself against it.

'I've been seeing it in my daydreams and in my nightmares for six days. These boats weren't built to cross the lake. But if you build them with a keel to cross the lake they can't navigate the river. Love and marriage, you might say.'

'And it looks so beautiful,' she said. 'So temptingly beautiful.'

'And so it was.'

'Love or marriage?'

'I was thinking of my first trip . . . '

And talking, remembering, he was on watch crossing the lake for the first time, coming from Hay River, a new deckhand who didn't know a marlin spike from a bollard. And Big Island was green and mysterious north of little Lobstick. And westward, inside Lobstick, lay Beaver Lake and the entrance to the Mackenzie, a sheet of water five miles wide and twenty miles long. A plain of water on which the first motion of the current would begin to give him his ride into a new and simpler wilderness.

On the islands the Indians were camped, smoke rising blue from their fires in front of tents. Canoes lined the beaches; fish were drying on racks: whitefish and lake trout and inconnu. Beaver Lake was polished a silver-blue as far as the pink sky of evening and the purple hills, and near at hand the rising fish drew circles on the water like raindrops on a pond. Ahead of the boat a loon dived, surfaced, dived again when the boat approached, and he remembered trying to guess where the quick black head would surface next; he guessed wrong each time and thrilled to this new unknown within an unknown. Beyond the loon a flock of swans rose out of a bay, their white wings throwing back the late sun. Ducks and geese and cranes rose up and circled, and when the boat had gone by settled down again and disappeared as if they had never been.

And when the forward barge hit a mudbank Peter discovered that the only channel through Beaver Lake was narrow and tricky; only a man with experience and judgment, who could read the meaning in a shade of colour, who could grip the wheel and guess his way below the surface — only he could take the heavily loaded barges through. The barge-loads of mining equipment and alkylate and lumber and clothing and dynamite and beer and foodstuffs for another year. He decided he must know this river, right to where in one last extravagance it flung all its beauty and violence and power and mystery into the Arctic Ocean; he would serve his apprenticeship and become a pilot.

'And the best one,' Kettle said.

Peter laughed. 'If you don't count a few Lepines and Bouviers and Bonnet Rouges and Laffertes, not to name Berens.' He lay looking up at the clear autumn sky. It might have been the sky of a football afternoon, clear and cool and smelling of frost and dry leaves. 'There'll be other boats next year. If I want them.'

'If you want them,' Kettle said.

'The chief and the skipper and Pottle can work on the coast or somewhere else. I'm stuck with this river. This is it.'

'But I'm leaving. I'm starting over brand new. My house is brand new. The trees are brand new. The fence is brand new. Even the lawn — it arrived one day while we were eating lunch.' Kettle gestured out at the stunted spruce and the moss. 'You should drop by, Peter. Just to see my brand new world. People come by to see it all the time.'

'But I'd track in the old world,' Peter said. 'I'd mess it up. I'd bring in Yellowknife, and the Old Town part with its bums and the jumble of shacks on the rock. Logs and tarpaper and false fronts and unpainted boards. And water waiting. There you'd be, raising your kids to be civilized, and in I'd come reeking of whisky or vanilla extract, and I'd say stake me one more time and I'll make you a fortune. I know where there's gold.'

'And would you find me gold, Peter?'

'I'd find you tons of gold. No, I'd find you champagne. I'd go to the bush and rocks and come back with champagne. Cases and cases. Just to make you happy. And we'd sit on your new lawn under a new tree and we'd drink champagne and be happy. If we just had one glass now we could start. We could call one of these a new tree. We'd drink and be happy.'

Kettle raised in her hand an imaginary glass. 'To drink and be happy.'

'To your new world.'

'To my new world, Peter.'

Peter started to drink. 'Don't spill it,' he said. 'Be careful.'

She turned and buried her face in his parka.

'You spilled it,' he said. 'It's all spilled.'

She lay on his parka. 'We'll have champagne,' she said. 'Won't we, Peter? We'll have champagne.'

'It makes the old world new,' he said. 'We have to have champagne.' He brushed imaginary drops of champagne off his parka and let his fingers touch her hair.

She shook his hand away, crying. 'No, Peter. Break the mirror for me. Break it, break it please, smash it, Peter. Listen to me, smash it.'

He put down his imaginary glass. He sat looking out beneath the trees at the distant water.

They left Lobstick Island at six p.m. It was a dark night, but the sky was clear and the water was calm. At eight o'clock, on his radio sked, the skipper learned that a cold front was moving in off the Barrenlands. The low temperature predicted for the night was one below zero. Already in Yellowknife Bay, the operator at the other end reported with some pride, the ice was four inches thick and dogteams were crossing from the Indian village.

They were pushing the two barges; there was just enough swell to keep the lines and the pushing posts creaking in the background as the crew gathered in the pilot-house. The light was on. The skipper was steering by compass, the indicator hand steady and the boat rolling just a fraction as she throbbed forward. The skipper told Peter he should get to bed early, regardless of whose bed he was going to sleep in. The last few miles into Yellowknife would be difficult; on top of the series of treacherous reefs, they would have ice to smash their way through.

'I'll run across that bloody ice,' Pottle said, 'with one of these barges for a schooner, and I'll head for that beer-parlour that's open night and day. And for the first forty-eight hours I'll sit right there with my boots off in front of two tables covered with beer.'

'And hundred dollar bills,' Louttit said. 'Aren't you going to eat one again? Like you did last fall?'

'It took two bottles of castor oil to move that damned thing, and I only got forty dollars back.'

'I'm not going to drink anything but a milkshake,' Mud said.

'What about that snort you promised us?' Louttit was sitting on the counter shuffling a deck of cards; no one would play him a hand of cribbage.

'After I listened to the chief, I'm finished. I'm never going to touch another drop.'

'He's in love, our lad,' Pottle said. 'Bless his soul, it isn't the chief at all at all. It's those pots of tea he keeps carrying up to Mrs. Hornyak. And God only knows what he does in that cabin.'

Mud blushed. 'She gets thirsty all by herself. She's an old married woman.'

'Those widows are the best thing.' The skipper looked up from the compass and winked toward everyone except Mud.

'She's a lady,' Mud said. 'She wouldn't do anything like that.' Mud was all scrubbed clean and Louttit had attempted to trim his hair.

'How the hell are we going to get you fixed up in Yellow-knife,' Pottle said, 'if you start talking like our cook?'

'I don't think you get yourself fixed up,' Mud said. 'I think you're just bragging, Pottle. You never had a dose in your life.'

Everyone laughed at Pottle's expense. 'Well I won't be bragging tomorrow night,' he said. 'I'll be doing it.'

'When you aren't in the beer-parlour,' Louttit said.

'I swore off women and I meant it.' Pottle crossed his heart and touched wood. 'They lead a man to nothing but grief. Just look at Arnafson. Or Hornyak out there.' He pointed out at the first barge. 'You lads follow me and you'll be on the straight and narrow.'

'But not tomorrow noon,' McAlpine said, 'when we see those old headframes against the sky. I'll need somebody to tie up this boat.'

'A smudge of real smoke on the horizon.' Mud gave a big sigh. 'And some second-hand cars for sale.'

'Taxis,' Pottle said. 'Taxis lined up and waiting. And gold in the streets. And whisky flowing from all the taps. The gold-en knife, me b'ys. The glittering knife of gold.'

'And you forgot the ravens,' Louttit said. 'The good old ravens flapping around, stealing the caps off beer bottles and the balls off the golf course.'

'They've had snow,' the skipper said. 'You're a damned bunch of fools. They've got snow in Yellowknife, two inches and more.'

126

'Not for me, they haven't,' Pottle said. 'It's all sunny and clear to me. The colour of a season's wages. Green and gold like money. And everything that money will buy, including an airplane ride to wherever you want to go.' He did a jig and went to the pilot-house door. 'A turkey sandwich, anyone?' Then he opened the door and stepped outside. 'Looks a little dark out here, skipper; better step on it, b'y.'

The wind came up at four in the morning, rather suddenly, when they were somewhere off Edgar Point. A cloud loomed out of the north-east, blacker than the night, and was upon them by the time they rigged the bridles and lines and dropped the two barges and had them out on tow. A gust of wind rocked the high pilot-house of the shallow-draft and flat-bottomed boat when they turned across the rising waves to pick Louttit off *309;* he had stayed aboard to get the bridle ready, so the barge would tow straight, and to keep the heavy line clear of the boat's propellers.

'It'll slow us down a bit,' the skipper said, 'but once the front has moved by we should be okay.'

Peter was rubbing the sleep out of his eyes. 'You should have called me earlier.'

'We'll need you soon enough. Once we get to the reefs.'

Peter stepped to the rear of the pilot-house to look down on the stern. The deckhands were standing by the winch and the winch engine; still paying out line. They were hunched against the cold wind, looking pale and chilled in the raw glare from the stern floodlight. 'By God, there's a little snow falling,' Peter said. Traces of snow laced the bright light.

'That time of year,' the skipper said.

The two deckhands held on to the lifeboat or the winch as the boat came into the wind and the pitching increased. Louttit looked up at the pilot-house.

'About six hundred feet of line out,' Peter said, 'by the look of the winch drum.'

'That'll do.'

Peter signalled through the window and Louttit set the brake on the winch and Mud turned to help Pottle lash down the washing-machine.

'I'll do a stint,' Peter said. 'Maybe you can catch a little shut-eye.'

'I'm wide awake,' the skipper said. 'Anxious to get there, I guess.'

By dawn they could see only the blizzard, punctuated by the heave of a wall of water that shuddered the whole boat each time the flat-bottomed bow made its plunge. A gale was blowing. The compass swung wildly each time the boat rolled. The thermometer outside the chief's cabin read two below zero.

They had to keep a pilot-house window open; the spray that swept the whole boat froze as it touched. A half-inch of ice coated the closed windows. It coated the bow and the decks; behind the wheelhouse it polished the stack and the winch and the cover on the lifeboat. It turned the deckhands' slickers into shining armour. It sealed the entrance to the forecastle.

By nine o'clock a half-inch line hanging down off the bitt on the bow was four inches thick with ice. The deckhands went out with fire axes and when Mud first knocked a chunk of ice off the rail it skidded down the deck like a curling rock and slammed the mate off his feet. 'Like a kick with a frozen boot,' he shouted into the wind. 'Abraham should be here,' Mud shouted. 'We could use him.' 'He was too damned popular with himself to get wet.' And the waves smashing at the bow, the spray sweeping over the ninety-foot length of the boat, formed new ice as fast as the old was chopped away.

Peter at the wheel had his face drenched with freezing water. Snow swirled into the pilot-house. He was braced between the wheel and the wall to keep from being knocked down as the pilot-house swung and jerked back; his arms were beginning to ache though the skipper spelled him every twenty minutes.

Out behind they could seldom see the first barge. Now and then as its shovel-nosed bow slapped into a wave the spray, coming away as if shot from a gun, was visible as a burst of white more intense than the snow. The second barge, with the reefer, they could only assume was out somewhere behind the first.

When no cook appeared the mate went looking and found her frozen into her cabin, knocking furiously at the inside of the door. A deckhand broke the ice away with an axe so the door could be opened and the two men managed to get her into the galley. She put the rolling rails on the stove, the men already gone to other jobs. Peter had come down from the pilot-house for a drink of something warm and was closing a port-hole; water sloshed on the deck. At her first attempt to pour coffee-grounds into a pot both Angi and the pot were hurled across the galley. She was trying to get a pot of soup to stay on the stove when the door to the engine-room opened and the din from the engines was added to that of the boat crashing through waves. Then the chief was hanging onto an overhead I-beam and trying to tell Peter something. His face was an ashen-grey and sweating and Peter clung to the same beam and put his ear to Arnafson's mouth. 'Tell the skipper. Go tell the skipper. The tunnels are leaking. Over the screws. From the hammering they're taking. The bilge-pumps can't handle it. They're losing ground. We can't last two hours out here.'

Peter left and ran and dodged and crawled to the pilot-house on the slippery and heaving decks. The cold steel and the ice stiffened his fingers. His boots were glossy with ice when the wind slammed the door at his heels.

Mud was at the wheel for the moment. The skipper was on the radio, trying to get a weather report from anyone who happened to be listening.

'We've got to go back,' Peter said.

The skipper frowned and pointed at the squealing radio.

'We've got to get to an anchorage! I think without the tow we could make Hardisty Island!'

129

'We can't drop the tow,' the skipper shouted. 'It'll blow hell and gone across the lake.'

'The chief says –' Peter braced himself as the boat slammed into the next wave. 'Arnafson says the bilge-pumps can't handle it. The tunnels are leaking –' Then he ducked away from the open window as the spray came high over the wheel-house. Mud ducked too late and was soaked again. He sput-tered like a swimmer and clung to the wheel.

'We've got to get rid of that damned tow. It's taking us with it.' Peter raised his voice. 'And it looks like the wind is switch-ing. To the north-west. Maybe we can still run with it to Hardisty.'

The skipper returned to the radio, his legs straddled so he wouldn't be knocked over. 'This is the *Nahanni Jane*. This is the *Nahanni Jane*. *Nahanni Jane* calling. We are somewhere off Edgar Point. We are icing up badly. This is the *Nahanni Jane*. *Nahanni Jane* to Yellowknife. *Nahanni Jane* to Yellow-knife. How do you read? How do you read? Come in please, Yellowknife. Over.'

He let go of the switch on the microphone and the crackle of static filled the pilot-house. He reached swaying and turned a dial and for a crazy moment a burst of Dixieland filled the air. Peter had to shout over the whistling radio: 'We've got to cut the tow-line, skipper. Let the barges go. They're both empty and sealed. You couldn't pile enough ice on one to sink it.'

Pottle banged into the pilot-house in a swirl of snowflakes. 'I left the ocean, by God. Because I get seasick at the sight of an egg-beater. And here I am riding out a big blow in a blast-ed bloody washtub.' He knocked the snow and ice out of his red hair and was in turn almost knocked over. He steadied himself against the wheel. 'Skipper, that ice out there is get-ting too heavy. We ain't coming up fast enough out of the waves.'

'It's Hardisty Island in two hours,' Peter said. 'Or the near-est shelter is fifty miles away. And that's too far.'

'The old *Northern Trader*.' Pottle pulled off his stiff gloves

and blew into a closed fist. 'She went to pieces at Burnt Island, and she thought she was in a shelter. And we sit out
here like this bleeding bloody thing is a submarine.'

'It's that damned wind changing,' Peter said.

Mud looked up from the compass. 'Skipper, I think I got
to throw up.'

'Okay.' The skipper turned down the radio. 'Goddamnit, okay.
Get me the body off that barge and cut them loose. We'll let an
airplane find them.'

'I think I should throw up,' Mud said.

'Well throw up, goddamnit.' The skipper went out on deck.

'Don't throw up unless you want to,' Pottle said. He switched
off the radio. 'And don't throw up all over that compass.'

Louttit was on the stern burning rags soaked in bunker to
keep the steering gear from freezing up. A foot of ice coated
the low stern. Louttit kept looking around, dodging the tow-
line, and the skipper caught his attention and signalled him
up to the pilot-house.

'You're out of your mind.' Pottle met the skipper at the
door.

'We can do it, goddamnit. If we have to.'

'We can shit worms with cowbells. But who *wants* to.'

'It's in the canoe.' The skipper swayed backwards and was
almost gone out the door when Pottle caught the front of his
coat. 'When our bow hits two men jump aboard the barge
and then when the stern swings in to hit they push the canoe
over like a sled and jump after it.'

'We're going up and down like a yo-yo,' Pottle said, 'and
the barge will be doing the same.'

'But they've got to be level for a moment. You've put those
two barges on tow in something as bad.'

'For a better reason, goddamnit, skipper. A corpse is something to be buried.'

They began to argue and McAlpine took the wheel from
Mud. He started the turn. The wind was changing fast enough
so that it was crossing the waves.

131

'I think we should just let go,' Peter said. He pointed back through the snow. 'The way that tow-line is going slack, we could catch it in the wheels or the rudders. Then we'd be done.'

'One try,' McAlpine said. 'We can't sail into Yellowknife and say we didn't try. Tell that to a bunch of high-collars sitting in a warm office.'

'In a couple days,' Pottle said. 'A helicopter could get it off.'

'I won't say I didn't try. I can't lose my ticket just because you — '

'Look out!' Mud screamed. 'A rock!'

'An island!'

The skipper grabbed at the telegraph.

A white and black blur. It loomed in the grey-white of the blizzard. And then the rock or island was *Barge 301* with the reefer aboard, and 'He's come!' the mate yelled, and still they were moving toward it; a wave towered black above them and the barge was gone and then the water crashed over them and they were almost on top of the wind-carried barge, and 'Quick!' the skipper was shouting, his only order, and the mate had his two deckhands down on the bow in the freezing spray and he cursed and raised an eye of wire to loop over a bollard on the deck of the barge that came snow-covered at them and now it was time he dropped the eye, caught a bollard, but as he tried to fasten his line to the bitt the barge went down, down below them riding down on a wave, the deck below them, then the reefer, then the reefer's roof below them and the bow of the boat rising and 'Get ready!' the skipper was shouting against the gale, 'Get ready to jump!' and Peter at the top of the ladder saw the two deckhands go to the sides of the bitt on the bow, one on either side of Pottle, and then he saw the barge hesitate in its plunge and as it started to rise he knew it was coming too fast for young Mud and he himself dropped, slid down the rails of the ladder on his two hands and ran forward and as the barge came up, the boat high in the sky and poised and all of a sudden dropping he saw Mud hesitate

132

and he ran and hooked a leg over the rail on the bow, poised his weight, and then a voice from behind him, Kettle, soaking wet, clinging to the ladder he had just come down, 'Don't! Forget him, for God's sake!' and then the barge came up, was there, waiting, and he jumped and an instant later the pushing-post on the other side smashed against the barge and broke off and was hurled across the deck and he heard Louttit scream and saw him spin back onto the boat and then the boat was gone, the bow dropping down and he was high, high in the air and snow and high and alone as if on a cloud and he staggered and clutched the rising deck as it met him and as the barge began its next fall he was alone he felt and floating alone on the air.

They were swinging around to pick him up. To pick up him or the body. As he came to he saw the old boat coming around, but staying too long in the trough, awkward, too much water in the bilges, too heavy with ice. She would take the next wave over the stern, and after that she couldn't take another and he was crawling, staggering; he caught hold of the capstan and stood up and signalled: Don't try it again, I'm okay. He danced and waved his arms to show he was fine and he signalled, waved with both hands as if to push, to drive them on, the boat still hesitating, the skipper hesitating at the wheel. And then he ran to the starboard bollard and lifted off the bridle with a savage hoist and it snapped out of his hands. He ran skidding on the ice to the port side, the barge already yawing, and he waved, pointed: that way to Hardisty Island. The bridle came off. And then the boat was swinging, starting to turn away, heavy, listing, and someone released the brake on the winch and the boat was away and leaping forward. Someone stepped out of the pilot-house and waved, briefly, a reassuring wave, a promise, the boat already disappearing into the storm.

And he was alone on the barge and the swirl of snow was
all about him. He faced into the slashing snow and went to
the door of the reefer. But he stopped at the closed door and
turned away and walked around to the sheltered side and
hunched into the shed that covered the reefer motor. All he
needed was a piece of tarpaulin. Something to cover him. The
barge was swept clean of everything but ice and snow and the
reefer. Not a gangplank, not an empty drum or a line or a
rag remained aboard. Only the reefer and the splintered pushing-post. He crouched in the shelter of the reefer, needing
only a few yards of old tarpaulin. He started again for the
door of the reefer but settled back against the leeward wall
and the snow swirling out of the storm touched him white
now, the flakes not blinking away as they did when they hit
the waves, not swept along as they were on the open deck of
the barge. His head ached. He had hit himself a blow on the
side of the head when he jumped and fell. He half dozed but
woke up as the pitch of the barge threatened to sprawl him
out flat and he stood up and clapped his hands and jumped
but then stopped trying and sat down, hunched down, and
he knew he should get the tarpaulin and argued, Let me in,
Hornyak. Get out of there.

'Where to hell do you think you're going?'

'West.'

'Jump in.'

'You're headed east.'

'Christ, Hornyak can turn this jalopy around.'

Where he stood in the hot sun by the sign that said 'WEL-
COME TO MANITOBA'. A calm hot afternoon. And he was welcome for three hours. While every so often a car whizzed by,
breaking the speed limit. A Pontiac, a Ford, a Dodge; he count-
ed the empty seats. Two hundred even. Eighty cars. Two and
a half empty seats to a car. He figured it out. Twenty-six and
two-third cars going his way every hour. One car every two
and a half minutes. He figured it out, and the birds chattered
and didn't know and didn't care.

And then this crazy Hornyak came along and they were

tearing west, 'WELCOME TO MANITOBA WHITESHELL PROVINCIAL PARK'; and they tore through the hot sun, the glare in their eyes, tore west from that rock outcrop and the white on green sign that promised 'WINNIPEG 99 MILES'. West on Highway One they went, west on One, through the hard-rock cuts, a straight road but up and down, like the roll of waves; a straight-through road, but instead of a park they found a burnt-off country; miles of tree-trunks – black, gaunt, crooked – the ground strewn with boulders and rock. And the sun blazing down and all the time, out there ahead, the prairies. 'Chaos,' Mike said. 'We've got some chaos to contend with. So hand me that bottle under your seat.' He drank and said, 'Contend a little?'

Peter contended. He was twenty years old and scared. And they boomed west, and he talked about the girl he was going to see. Talked frantically.

'Chaos, boy. Stay young and hang loose.' And Mike fed more gas to the wild horses under the hood of that black Rolls.

And the flat country then. Dusty and dry. Dry and dusty and hot. Wheat country. And the first elevator. There at Dufresne, alone and reaching, like a great damned phallus, like one perpetual hard-on, Mike said, trying to make eternity. They laughed and the sky was so big that Peter couldn't breathe. He hadn't believed there was so much sky. And trees looking self-important and a little scared. The high piercing whine of gravel trucks. And little gas-station cafés that looked like boxes that fell off the roaring semi's that shook the trees and the telephone-poles.

They raced a train outside Ste. Anne. The track a bee-line of steel. Silver coaches with purple trim, blue windows in the high observation car where the stony faces sat air-conditioned and out of the dust, staring down at a sunless blue world.

They passed the old Model A's converted into pick-ups, caught the smell of hogs or wheat, passed the Mercurys and the VWs and the sunburnt arms in the open windows, the new Jags and MGs that the farm boys tried to screw in.

Groves of poplar and white barns off on either side, afloat in the heat. And the black dirt parched and the green grass going brown too early, and a wheat train drew a horizon and the two trains whistled and blurred across each other in the sun.

And the bunk-houses of the road-building gangs. 'Build us lots of highways,' Hornyak shouted. Over the diesel and gravel roar. The smell of tar. To dusty-faced men on cats and tractors, men swinging picks and pouring cement and laying asphalt. 'Build them right out into Georgia Strait.'

And two big Grey Goose buses came at them through the hanging dust with their lights on and Hornyak rode the white line and they swerved and he cheered: 'You got to believe, boy, you got to believe in something.' 'I'm trying to,' Peter said.

And a big red ESSO sign and E

A

T the neon blaze commanded.

'I'm starving,' Hornyak said. 'I'm a starving man. Watch for a sign.'

They bought three bottles of burgundy. They found a store. They bought food. Mike bought food. They carried oranges and melons and cheese and bologna and bread until the back seat was a supermarket. They drove to a roadside park. And every time a car stopped they asked the people to join them, and everyone laughed and brought out potato salad and baked beans and big chocolate cakes and strawberries and cream and fresh rhubarb pies. They drank the wine. Then cases of beer tumbled out of the trunks of cars like rabbits out of a hat. More people stopped. The traffic snarled and a policeman drove up and they gave him a beer and he took off his hat to wipe the sweat-band and drank the beer and ate some ice cream that was going soft in the dying heat. 'The land of promise,' Hornyak told him. 'The land of opportunity. Don't let the cars pass us up.' And they sang hymns; Mike stood on a table full of dirty plates and led and they all waved their beer bottles and sang a few hymns and 'Home on the Range' and 'Glory, Glory, What a Hell of a Way to Die'. And then Peter whispered, 'I've got to keep moving.'

'Just hang loose a minute, boy. Just pass me one of those chilled brown bottles. Just wait and see.'

And in the dawn he woke up with a pain in his head. He shook Mike out of the front seat, and Mike went to find water. But the pump wouldn't pump.

They jarred themselves into the morning. The tires spat gravel onto the orange peels and the melon rinds. They hit the new black-top with a bounce, 'PROCEED WITH CAUTION KEEP RIGHT', and Hornyak reached under the seat and brought out the sorry remains. 'No use breaking this damned thing.'

St. Boniface, then, and rows of railway tracks and a sign 'ENJOY PEPSI' and the radio in the car saying 'CKRC for the young of heart'. 'You've got to keep young,' Hornyak said, half as a joke, half desperate. 'That's the whole secret, boy.'

And remembering an old brick house in Ontario and china in the windows. A story for every cup. A fence out back; a stone fence older than the house; as old as a farm that was older than the town. Apple trees and oak trees gone crooked with age. The stories his mother told, of apple trees and fences; of the spring-time of the dead.

Mike looked at all the licence plates as he whipped by. The colours and numbers and slogans and signs. A little bison. 'Wheat Province'. A potato. 'Tradition,' Mike said. 'It's an old tradition of mine to have breakfast at noon. Let's stop somewhere and start my old tradition.'

Portage Avenue was gaudy and wide; the traffic lights bloomed red and green. 'It's too early for your old tradition,' Peter said.

The wind whipped his shirt against his chest. Fingers of wind in his blond hair. He leaned forward and the sweat ran down his spine. And he stuck to the genuine leather saddle while the wild horses drank gas and in Portage la Prairie he said, 'There's hope here.' He pointed to a flaming billboard: 'Ye cannot *repent* your life; but ye can *repent* your sin.'

'There's hope, but not much,' Mike said. 'I just want some water.' And on to the Moosomin beer-parlour, for some hair of the dog. Past a load of baled straw upset off a truck. Past snow-fences rotting in the sun.

And then they saw it: a little wooden town and a reckless sign: 'The Best Water in Manitoba'.

'It's a disguise,' Mike said. 'This is it. The eternal fountain.' He rejoiced with both hands in the air. And swung the Rolls into town on four screaming tires.

They knocked with a big brass knocker at the door of a big white house and asked for a drink of the best water in Manitoba and a woman in shorts and curlers wouldn't unhook the screen and said she'd wake her husband if they didn't leave at once.

And then out onto the farmlands again and the wind had its own sound; forlorn, sad to the limits. And far beyond it Kettle was in the cool mountains and bright in a summer dress, the air cool and the rain falling in the afternoon and the sun coming out again after the rain.

They drove. Past oilfield pumps, like giant grasshoppers dying of thirst. Past farmers making hay in the ditches. Past cars with racks on top and tarpaulins flying and trailers swaying behind. All of them heading west. Mike whistled past in the Rolls he called his jalopy. And then stopped for milkshakes or beer, and the cars went by again, the same luggage piled high on the same racks and the same tarpaulins flapping. 'Water,' Hornyak said. Their bellies ached from too many pineapple milkshakes. 'I'm a walking living drought. There must be water out there ahead.'

And for thirty miles they followed a car that was pulling a boat on a trailer. The car stopped for gas and they pulled up too. 'Pass,' the boatman said. 'If you want to pass, pass. And learn to drive while you're at it.' 'But we don't want to pass,' Mike said. 'Where's the water?' 'Wise guy,' the boatman said. 'The *water*,' Mike said. He pointed back at the dust on the boat. 'The *water*. Where the hell's the *water*?' The boatman laughed and laughed. 'That's a good one,' he said. He picked some thistles out of his grill. 'Where the hell's the water! That's a damn good one, buddy.'

And just before Elkhorn the microwave tower sending the invisible word. And two Indians waiting for a ride. Mike gave them a lift for twenty miles and they didn't speak a syllable but leaned forward over the back seat and watched the speedometer and didn't say thank you and didn't move when they got out but were standing there by the roadside as the Rolls boomed around the next bend.

And into Saskatchewan and off to the right going west from Grenfell a sea of green wheat; it hurt their eyes to look out to the edge; and granaries sitting out there like some kind of silly boats and windbreaks green on the coral farms. And the wind blowing. Always a hint of the wind.

'We're lost,' Mike said.

They kicked up the dust in front of some gas-pumps in Swift Current. Four people were waiting for a bus: an ancient Chinaman and two elderly ladies and a young girl with a big, worn, cheap suitcase that looked borrowed and a new hair-do that she had to protect from the wind. She jumped out of a car and tried not to cry and ran to catch the bus, waving and laughing and crying as she went up the steps, her suitcase getting in the way. The door closed. 'Yuh,' Peter said. 'That's it. It's like that, Mike.'

The attendant wiped the bugs off the windshield and Mike thanked him and told him to keep the change and he looked at the six dollars in his hand as if it might explode.

'We're lost,' Mike said.

The attendant was doing the windshield again and he let his jaw drop and pointed to a sign: 'REGINA 42 MILES'.

'No,' Mike said. 'We're lost.'

He must explain to Kettle. In the Old Town, over champagne. He'd tell her. And all they could eat. His legs were weak from his hunger. We were delayed. He forced his eyes open: he concentrated against the light: the bow of the barge, the capstan black on the ice-sheathed bow, a chaos of water and sky. He could see only the storm; water and sky, confused in the tangle of snow.

But those prairie nights; we saw lakes and we drove and the lakes turned out to be sky.

We were delayed, Kettle. Delayed. Always the unexpected.

A gust of wind took his breath. He straightened away from the reefer, and doubled again, discovering his hunger. He must look for the boat. There were three chocolate-bars in the drawer under his bunk. Quick energy. So he could stand up. The chocolate stained a brownish white; one day in the summer the bars all melted. He couldn't eat them after that; the funny colour. He swayed as the barge pitched; his hands came out of his parka. He touched a hand to his eyes, to his cheeks. He was chapped and cold. He touched and wasn't sure he could feel. His fingers stiffened in the wind; he needed a glance in a mirror. To see if he was turning white. His cheeks grey-white and that funny gloss. The wind whipping his shirt and too much to drink in the afternoon and the road up and down.

'What're you going to be, Guy?'

'A lawyer, I guess. If I live through this.'

'A good guess, boy. Maybe you can keep me out of trouble. Sometimes I get into trouble, Guy. Just looking for water.'

'What're your plans, Mike?'

'You ever make it with a red-head, Guy?'

'Well, not really.'

'They're zealots, boy.'

The girl between them on the front seat had her hair dyed red. She giggled. They found the by-pass outside Regina and she said, 'Let's go all the way to Moose Jaw. You got money to burn, you guys.'

And the country flat to Moose Jaw and Peter drove for the first time, like all hell was on his tail. Past two big movie screens, looming on the young night. A herd of galloping horses on a Technicolor plain. And telephone-poles. A line of poles like scaffolds and the country flat and the road all theirs. The night all theirs.

And at Gull Lake a big H turns and turns on top of a big hotel. Turning and turning, an H red on one side, green on the other, like running lights; winding people in off the road. They drank beer at noon. And they looked for the lake at Gull Lake. 'Where's the water?' Mike pleaded to a man with a white walking-cane. 'It's dried and drained and gone,' the old man said. 'No lake and damned few gulls.' And the bartender laughed when they asked and he patted his change apron and wouldn't listen, and he ribbed a cowpoke for tracking cow-shit into the bar and the cowpoke up and flattened him with one swing. 'Dandy. The proper thing. Justice was served,' Mike said. 'Let us stand you a drink, sir.' But the cowpoke apologized for his undue haste and said he had to mosey along.

And west of Gull Lake no farms but parched hills and ranching country and rattlesnake country. Dry shortgrass and silver-blue sage, and green patches of buckbrush in the damp crevices of the hills. Small granite boulders here and there. The clack of grasshoppers and the dry squeak and rattle and whirr of insects in the brown ditches. Flowers with sticky yellow eyes that caught hungry bugs. And Mike gave the redhead one hundred dollars in Medicine Hat, insisted that she get back home, and he slapped Peter's shoulder:

'Well, you learned something, boy. All red-heads are not zealots.'

And back in the car Hornyak picked up the handful of road-maps and looked at all the red lines. The green parks and the blue rivers and the black highway numbers. The little mileage figures. 'This is the trouble,' he said. He pitched all the maps out his window. They zoomed out of town and flipped a coin at the next crossroads. They drove and Peter read a few signs, 'CAUTION PHEASANTS, ANTELOPE CROSSING, RAILWAY CROSSING'. 'No more of those damned signs, Mr. Guy.' And they boomed out past old tires on fenceposts and section

141

gangs sweating along the glare of hot steel. They lost count of the days, moving into quiet towns where the women watched the dust drifting into their wash. They stayed a day or a night, drinking too hard, and Peter wrote thirteen postcards and couldn't post them, and they drove on past sheep-herders' shacks and cowpokes fixing fences in the blaze of sun. And already the spring heat was drying the sloughs; the nesting ducks found their feet getting muddy. And they drove and pitched beer bottles, dropping an arm from an open window and pitching the bottles so they arced up and over; arced over the car, high and gentle and spinning in the bright air, and gently falling into the far ditch, the car already gone.

They drove and drank, their fury turned sullen. Quiet. Subdued. Almost defeated. They drank and drove and when their bladders ached they stopped; they were standing by the road pissing away out on the alkali-stained prairie, helping nature, Hornyak said. And two girls from Montana in a roadster went by laughing and tooting their horn, a sign on their bumper in phosphorescent orange: 'YE MUST BE BORN AGAIN'.

'I cheated,' Mike said. 'I read it.'

'I was peeking myself,' Peter said.

They jumped into the Rolls and pulled up beside the roadster doing eighty and Mike shouted: 'Did you like what you saw? Would you like a better look?'

Both cars slowed down. And two days and one night in jail later Mike and Peter were back on One and into Calgary and hearing the jackhammers sing again.

'Banff,' Peter said. 'The road to the mountains. God, I am all one ache for the mountains.'

'Ah, Guy, my lad,' Hornyak said. 'Women. They keep us young. The girls from Calgary will keep us young.'

They followed the Calgary girls, driving lead-footed for the Rockies on a Saturday morning, range after range of foothills as they topped a rise, up and up from the prairies, past all the hay-fields and into the forest and then the first outcrop of rock and the first mountain stream and the first lake. 'Water,'

Hornyak said. 'Dear sweet God, water.'

And the park gate: 'Two dollars, please. Have you any guns?'

'No, ma'am,' Peter said.

'Yes, ma'am,' Hornyak said. 'Two. Loaded.'

And the streets were full of women. Office girls from Toronto who stepped long-legged out of glass buses and girls from Montreal with little gold crosses on their bare bosoms and brown-thighed girls from California who rode up the mountains in white Cadillacs.

And then at the Banff Springs Hotel, at The Springs, they found Kettle.

Hornyak held his breath for a long time and then he said slowly, 'You lucky bastard. No wonder you didn't mind. When we drove like maniacs. When the cops couldn't catch us even, that night outside MacLeod. No wonder you wouldn't sleep in the morning. And how do you do, Miss Fraser?'

She was beautiful. Her lips and her breasts and God she was beautiful; her pale blue dress neatly ironed, her shoulders newly tanned; and her ears that the sun dared not touch and her black hair piled in a coil and her body slim in the cool morning. 'The mountains,' Peter said. 'I hadn't seen the mountains before.'

'You must see the mountains,' she said. 'I've seen nine days of mountains.'

They drove in Hornyak's jalopy. They went to Lake Kananaskis and watched the divers in their skunk-suits plunging deep and out of sight in the green-blue water. And they smelled the trees. After all those prairie nights they smelled the spruce, the pine. They looked at the Indian teepees and the cars parked out front. At the buffaloes in their paddock. They drove to Lake Louise, the forest at attention on its tall thin legs as they wheeled for the glacier.

'Who are you?' she said to Peter. 'Is Mike the stranger or are you?' 'I came a long way to find you,' he said. But she wouldn't let him kiss her; they screamed around a corner and onto the last climb to Lake Louise and its flowers and ice.

And that afternoon they found the stream. The water pouring down the mountain, past the Upper Hot Springs pools. Hot and smelling of sulphur, from somewhere high on the cold mountain. Two old women were sitting on a towel, soaking their swollen feet.

'Look,' Peter said. 'Those two old ladies. We saw them get on the bus.'

'This is it!' Mike shouted. He slammed on the brakes. 'We've found it! Quick! Get out!' And he left the Rolls in the middle of the road, horns honking. 'Run!'

They took off their shoes. They sat with their feet in the hundred-degree water in the sunlight on the mountain-side. The smell of pine and spruce over the smell of sulphur. Kettle with her dress up past her knees and Peter grinning and Hornyak kneeling in the spring, trying to get closer.

And when they started to sing, to laugh, a wrinkled old man who couldn't die came out from behind a rock wall: 'Take your feet out of that damned water.' Which made them stop singing. He yelled again and ignored the two old women and shook a fist and started down the hill. And they took their feet out of the water. They wiped them on Mike's and Peter's socks and put on their shoes and brushed their seats.

'You're supposed to pay. Up there,' the guard called.

'You can't pay,' Mike yelled back. 'Not to be reborn.'

And the three of them felt robbed. Cheated. Sad to the limits.

'I need a little rest,' Kettle said. 'It's the mountains, I guess. The altitude and the high air.'

'I'll see about my job,' Peter said.

'I'll run Kettle back to the hotel.' Mike touched his unshaven face. 'Maybe we can do something tonight. Or maybe I'll hit the road.'

And that evening with a contract in his pocket and a promise of work in the morning, Peter walked into her room; cracked

144

the door, afraid she was asleep; looked in on a mirror and the image of two raging bodies, a tumble of dark hair. And he was caught. He fled and fled and was caught there, trapped, doomed in that long mahogany frame. He fled and went on searching and could not see himself. Stay out, the voice said. Peter? the voice said. And he jerked at the handle; he braced himself and pulled, all his hunger black in his stomach. Who killed him, Peter? Who did it, finally? And he was still too weak. Too stiff with the cold. He hit the door with a wooden fist, struck the frozen lock with his bleeding hand and jerked again. And the door burst open; the two-by-fours in neat rows overhead, the meat-hooks empty. Stay out, the voice said.

But he had to look. He had to see that face, bear-touched and broken. The young face bleached to whiteness. This time he had to look.

The frayed end of a once expensive tie.

And the strength born of his heard laughter: the body toppled stiff from the canoe; hit the water; was lost in the snarl and riot of waves. He did not lock the door, and wrapped in the quilt and tarpaulin he lay in the small canoe. Curled in the quilt and tarpaulin he heard the slamming door, hour after hour. And as the huge door opened he saw the grey light of the blizzard, saw the glare and the snow and heard the plunge of wind and water, and as it closed he was slammed back into darkness again, the silence again, and the soft delirium of his impassioned motion.